MURMURS OF MAGIC

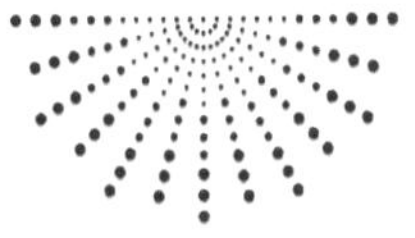

KIM JACKWAYS

REDFERNE WITCHES BOOK THREE

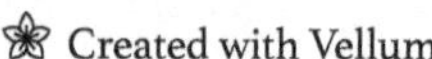 Created with Vellum

CHAPTER ONE

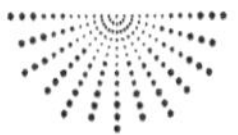

"Close the door!" Hazel called, as a freezing blast swirled through the room, flicking the pages over in the book she was reading. She tried not to imagine the chill wind bringing unseen creatures into the cottage.

She heard Joel's boots come off with a dull thud. He appeared from the hallway, grinning, and Bonnie wagged her tail on the ground a few times, but it was far too much effort to actually move from her spot by the fire.

Seeing his face gave Hazel a warm feeling and then a sudden chill as the images from her dream from last night flashed in her mind.

Cool air. That gritty feeling of a Batman movie. Concrete walls. Somehow, she knew she had followed Joel into a huge basement. It was half dark and one of the fluorescent lights flickered.

She could see reflections. Large panes of glass surrounded her, so that she felt she was in a zoo, and people were waiting for her next move, waiting for her to react. But who was watching her?

Joel felt far away, although they were only metres apart,

and she reached for him. He moved to the edge of her vision, and the next minute, slumped forwards.

Hazel shivered, and Bonnie raised her head to look over from her spot by the fire, as their familiar connection showed the dog Hazel's fear.

Dreams were tricky, shifting and mysterious, she knew that. It might be a symbolic representation. But Hazel wasn't about to disregard the dream entirely. Either way, watching your partner die in a dream casts a terrible energy over your entire day.

That unsettling feeling had continued at work, coming back to her when she was at the coffee machine, or alone in the supplies room, raising the hairs on the back of her neck.

"It's good to see you too," Joel said to her, coming in close, oblivious to what she was thinking. His hair was plastered to his head and his hoodie had dark wet patches on it. Cold drops fell from his hair onto her and she squeaked. He kissed her soundly, lips freezing cold on hers but gradually warming up. It took her a while to break it off.

"Go and dry yourself off by the fire," she said, putting her book down, and gesturing to the pot belly stove that was now roaring. "What have you been doing?"

"I've got a leak. The dripping was driving me mad. Thought I'd better go up on the roof and have a look." He lifted his socked foot up to bring it close to the fire. Bonnie immediately rolled over with a groan to take up the space, stretching her legs out.

"Careful with putting your foot down," she said to Joel. "Could the roof not have waited until tomorrow?"

He shook his head. "Not really. The house is made of wood so any moisture getting in is a real pain."

She sucked in her breath. "Well, I hope the rain will stop soon. Three days of it is enough."

"We're meant to get a small break in the weather in the morning," he said, looking for a spot to put his foot in around the dog. "How? How does she always manage to get the best spot? No matter what I do?"

"It's a very dark art that she excels in," Hazel said, shooting a look at her familiar.

Joel smiled, but he seemed very distracted. Pulling his hoodie off, he hung it on the fire guard to dry.

"What's up?" she asked.

He turned around slowly, and did his half smile. The couch creaked a little as he sat down next to where her feet were resting.

"You're reading me like a book again," he said. He reached across to cup her face with his rough hand. "Like always. I think I might have to get a loan."

"A loan? How come?"

"For the business. I am selling more chests through the website now," he said, taking her foot that was closest to him and lifting it over him to place it gently onto his lap. "And I'm selling some chopping boards and stools. Which is good, but I have to keep buying timber in the meantime to be able to keep up with it."

"That's great."

"It's all thanks to you. And I've got a few tools that need replacing too. They aren't cheap."

"No, I'd say they wouldn't be."

"A loan would help me get ahead," he said, pressing his thumbs into the soft flesh next to the ball of her foot through her sock. She let out a sigh. "Then I can focus on making the bloody things. Maybe I could even pay someone to help out, eventually. I actually called one of the smaller banks earlier. They want me to come in tomorrow."

She looked over his messy hair, and long sideburns. His

jeans had blades of grass clinging to them around the knee level, and his socks had a line of sawdust round the tops, where it must have fallen onto his boots.

"Mmm," Hazel said, eyes closed, as his warm hands moved across her foot. "Well, treat it like a job interview. Get a haircut, wear a nice shirt, clean your shoes."

"Yeah." He massaged around the edge of her foot, working his way up the outside until he got to her toes, which he squeezed, one at a time, before gently grabbing her ankle. She was still in her work clothes, black pants and a dark blue shirt, but she had let her hair down.

"I know I say this all the time," she said, "but everything is about the story. You can show them the money coming in from the chests."

"That is part of the problem. I've... kind of let the customers pay me later. Most of them I know, so it's fine."

"Oh." She frowned. She couldn't imagine the bankers thinking that was fine. "Then you could show them the emails with the orders. Don't make it difficult for them. Make it as easy as you can. Print them out before you go."

"That's not a bad idea," he said. He swung around and put his socked feet next to her on the couch, so they were facing each other. "I haven't got the best history with banks. As you know. I hope it's not all a huge waste of time." He didn't have to say he was feeling bad about it, and his feelings of anxiety and shame washed over her.

"You are not your past, though," she murmured. "You've been going so well. And everyone needs a second chance."

Life had been quiet for a few weeks, and they were spending a lot more time together. Hazel felt a deep contentment, as she traced the line of his jaw with her eyes; the shadow of stubble, his lips, down to his chest, his arms beneath his shirt sleeves. He had started going to the gym again, and she lingered over his biceps and forearms.

Bonnie shifted, and the shadows danced on the walls as a gust of wind came down the chimney. The dream came back to her in a sudden jolt, and she opened her mouth to tell him. But he looked at her then with such warmth that she didn't want to spoil the moment. She shook off the stupid feeling that saying it would make it come true.

"You can stay over if you like," she blurted, and flushed as hot as if she was next to the fire. "You know, so that you're warm and dry. That fire's hot once it gets going, isn't it?"

She got up to add another log to the fire, choosing a large piece of macrocarpa that would burn slowly.

"Stay on a school night?" he asked, stretching out on the couch. One corner of his mouth lifted.

"Well, why not? It's a Thursday night, which is pretty much Friday. You don't need to go home to check on the leak?" Hazel asked, walking back to him.

He shook his head. "Nah. It's not going to be any worse or better if I'm there. I'll stay right here. Warm and dry is good." His expression changed, and he reached for her.

Hazel woke first, and watched his face, the uncreased brow and slight curve of his lips as he slept without any of the worries of his waking hours. At least *his* sleep was peaceful.

She tried not to think of how his face had looked in the dream, equally as relaxed but without the life pulsing through it. He woke up and rolled towards her, blinking in the light through the white curtains. Then reached over with a lazy brush of his lips and a spike of stubble against her face. It was a reflexive, comfortable sort of movement.

"I'm heading over to have a look at the house first thing,"

he said, already pulling the covers back to get up. "See what the damage is."

"I'll come with you."

The day dawned fine but the trees were decorated with silver beads of water, and Hazel pulled on her gumboots as she went through the door. The steady trickle of a stream ran off the hill behind the house. She followed Joel through the gate to inspect the damage, and stopped to shut it, ducking under the bushes, which bent low with the weight of the water.

As she walked up to the cabin, she could hear Joel swearing, so she hurried in.

"Look at this!" He was pulling the furniture out from one of the corners and a dark patch of wetness was visible over his shoulder.

Hazel sighed. It didn't look good, and Joel's emotions were a storm of worry. He disappeared upstairs and called to her to grab the heater as he passed it down from the mezzanine. She caught it and put it down, but it would take a long time to dry and who knew how much damage it would do in the meantime.

"I should be able to... " She waved her hand and smiled. This was something she could help with.

"Oh right," he said, looking over, distracted and still plugging the heater into the wall. "Yeah, go on then."

Hazel concentrated all her energy into her hands and thought of the little drops of water soaking into the wood, imagining each one as a glass ball. She pulled on the air around the wet patch, gathering the water molecules slowly to her.

She tried to empty her mind, eyes closed. But the dark storm of his anxiety and worry crept into the corners of her mind, breaking her concentration.

"Sorry," she said, as the wetness spread around in a dark smudge.

"It got worse," Joel said. Hazel thought that was quite unnecessary. "I can deal with it," he added.

"No, just give me a second. Please. I have to clear my head a bit. Maybe if you go outside?"

He nodded and went out onto the deck. Hazel took a few deep breaths and pushed all thoughts that came into her mind firmly to one side.

"Can I come back in yet?"

"No," she called. "And try to be quiet."

This time she recalled her training, and the myriad ways she could clear her mind to make room for her powers. She made her mind into a cave and washed the tide out, taking with it any debris, expectations and worries that crept in like lurking goblins. Her mind was blank.

She looked back at the dark patch on the wall, noticing the fibres of the wood. She pulled with her hands, closing her eyes at the same time and breathed long and slow. She felt the water gathering above her palms, each tiny droplet adding to the shimmering pool. When she opened her eyes, Joel was peeking around the door, mouth open in surprise, and she got such a fright, that she jerked, sending the water up into the air and splashing on the floor, spattering her and Joel with drops.

She watched him, sensing to see if he was annoyed.

"Oh well, you tried." He pulled some towels out of one of the cupboards and began mopping up his face and the water on the floor.

"I had better get ready for work," she said, shaking the drops off her hoodie, "but I can try again later if you like."

He sat back on his heels. "You know, that was…"

She kissed him on the cheek. "I know," she said softly,

encompassing all the words that he couldn't say. Magic was amazing, mysterious, even frightening. It was all-consuming, and frankly, sometimes, just annoying. "See you later."

The office was filled with colour, as it was Hawaiian Shirt Day. It was part of Sia's latest team-building efforts. Hazel had found a red and blue shirt and wore it under her jacket. Because it wasn't exactly Hawaiian weather.

Sia had emailed them all to come to her desk for a quick, stand-up meeting. She sat back in her chair as everyone gathered around.

"Please come to the conference room first thing on Monday. We've got some big news around staffing," she said. "No, there won't be morning tea. June - be on time please. Matthew - no, we aren't getting rid of Perry. He's standing right there, geez."

Perry Strachan chuckled but Hazel could tell that it prickled.

"Something exciting next," Sia said. "We want to revamp Dunedin's image. We do this every few years. New tag lines. A whole new strategy."

She asked them to research how other cities marketed themselves. "Use the big international cities as a starting point and come up with some themes. In a week, we'll go over them."

A few groans came from around the table. Sia lifted a finger as if they were her children. "We'll reward the best ideas. There's an end-of-financial-year bonus pot we can dip into." She raised her eyebrows and looked at each of them in turn, long earrings jangling as she moved her head.

Everyone pretended not to be listening, but the energy

changed. One mention of the word 'bonus' and employees came out of the woodwork, gravitating towards the promise of money.

"How much will this bonus be?" Perry asked, leaning casually against the desk, a half-eaten muffin in one hand.

"We've got five grand put aside for it. Remember this is how Dunedin will be known to the rest of the country and international tourists for at least the next three years. It's big stuff."

Perry choked a little.

Hazel smiled. That amount could certainly come in handy. Perhaps it would be enough to help Joel out. It was time to get creative.

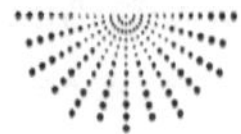

CHAPTER TWO

"*D*amn. I have to pop in to work." Hazel was browsing a book store with Joel when she remembered. How could she have forgotten the folder?

"Really? It's Saturday," he said, slipping his arm around her waist from behind and placing his head on her shoulder. "The weekend. You know, that thing where people rest and don't do any work?"

She nodded, running a finger over a beautiful embossed cover with a snake winding around it. Books were expensive here. Otherwise she would have a much larger collection at home.

"There is a competition in marketing. There's a nice little bonus riding on it," Hazel said, grabbing Joel's hand. "Honestly, it's important, otherwise I wouldn't bother."

It was a short walk in the brisk air until they arrived at the council offices, and her mind was working overtime. Something Sia had said had snagged at her thoughts. Why *were* they developing a new strategy? That normally only happened when there was a change in management.

She swiped her tag and the door opened with a beep.

"You can come in," she said to Joel, and he followed her inside, past the Reception desks.

"Are you sure I'm allowed back here?"

She cast an eye around the desks, which were mostly messy. A few half-deflated balloons from someone's birthday shout rested in the corner. She couldn't see anyone else. But why were the lights on?

"Back here? Yeah, it should be fine," Hazel said. She threaded between the desks to find hers. It was quiet after hours with the hum of the fans going in the background. Perhaps she could change her hours around so that she could do a weekend shift? No interruptions, no distractions. Her introvert soul would be completely happy.

"As long as you don't touch anything," she added, blocking Joel from touching the 3D printer. "That is so cool, isn't it? It's so that we can make promo objects like key rings..."

She shuffled through the papers, looking for the right one. Joel came up behind her. "Are there cameras up there?"

"Possibly," she said, distractedly, pulling out the grey folder from under her notepad. "Why?"

"There is *something* in here that I want to touch." He stepped in close, sliding his hand down her leg as she leaned over.

"Not here," she said, exasperated, although her heart had sped up.

"Why not? I could just be a colleague coming up behind to show you how to do something." His hands began to explore upwards as she straightened.

"First of all," Hazel said, turning around and slipping her arms around his waist. "It's normally me showing *them* how to do things. And second of all, no-one gets that close if they know what's good for them." She planted a kiss on his mouth. "Come on, let's get out of here."

They threaded their way back through the desks, until they came to the foyer, where light from outside made squares on the tiled floor. Hazel swiped to open the main door.

"What do you feel like eating?"

"Burgers?"

"That was quick," she said.

"I was already thinking about it," he laughed.

Behind them, the door dinged. Christo appeared, shading his eyes from the sunlight. He hadn't seen her yet, and Hazel debated hiding, but there was nowhere to hide. She put her hand awkwardly on her hip and stared into the distance.

"Oh, hello," he said, and she pretended to notice him with a start. Today he was wearing a reddish pink polo shirt and a navy cap. It was the first time she had seen him in anything but a suit.

"Gidday," she said, inwardly cringing. That was not how you greeted your boss.

Shit, he thought, as he walked past, and it floated to Hazel, clear as the traffic noise in the Octagon. *What is she doing here?*

As the doors started to shut, a hand reached out to stop them, then someone slipped through. She was slender and wearing sunglasses on her head, and a sleek navy sundress with a white sweater draped around her shoulders.

It wasn't until she passed them that Hazel realized who it was. Kirsten.

A shiver crawled up Hazel's spine. This was the same woman who had masterminded the sale of Joel's property. She had come to his house in order to steal the blood of the lizards to use in her potion. When Hazel had tried to stop her, she used some sort of suggestion magic to get her to do what she wanted, as well as attacking Bonnie. Later, Hazel found out that she was using the potion to manipulate other people, forcing them to do her bidding, in exchange for supply of the potion, which she called Confidence.

"Do you think those two are—" Joel murmured, lifting his eyebrows. "Y'know."

"Oh, I'm sure those two are. But I do not want to think about that. You know who that is, right? That's my boss. With that woman that bought your land."

"Oh right," he said, frowning. "I did think they looked familiar, but it's a small city. Everyone looks familiar."

"She is awful."

"Not this again."

"People are being taken in. Manipulated."

"Uh huh," Joel said, and she was sure he rolled his eyes. "Look, if it was really that bad, the police would be on it." He turned away and Hazel dropped it. Why did it feel like she was Cassandra and no-one was listening to her?

He might have faith in the police, but as an empath witch, Hazel had a different perspective. She had always heard cries for help floating in the air, and most of them were never confessed to anyone, let alone reported.

Take that man sitting on the cardboard box there with a bowl set in front of him. He would never be able to afford surgery for his cat, who was his one and only companion. He had been overflowing with silent pain since the cat limped back, a bullet having grazed its leg. Hazel glanced at him with sympathy.

She covered her eyes, peering up at the sky to see if it looked like rain later, but it seemed clear.

A feeling hooked her behind the eyeballs, as the sharp twin spires of the gothic St Paul's cathedral came into view.

She searched the building to see what had interested her. Some teenagers were sitting on the broad steps, looking at their phones.

As she looked, the bricks melted away from the top of the cathedral until only a quaint stone church remained on the hill. The kids were gone. The imposing wide steps of the cathedral had disappeared, and instead vines covered the stone bricks of a much smaller church. The sky seemed to darken with clouds wrapping dark fingers around the edges of her vision. Every cell in her body tingled.

"Did you see that?" she said breathlessly, turning to Joel.

Joel wasn't there. No, he was there — she could feel him. His hand was warm and firm in hers. But she could no longer see him standing next to her.

Instead, she was ankle deep in grass, and a small mound rose up to the south. It was a quiet and cool morning and fog hung over the harbour. Because it *was* Otago Harbour down there, with the peninsula curling around, although it looked so different. A dirt road ran past with saplings on either side and a path wound down the hill. A whiff of smoke floated in the air. Off to the side, the Robert Burns statue reclined in its black robes, watching over the whole peaceful scene.

Hazel stopped still as a woman picked her way down the path. She disappeared behind the hill, but Hazel couldn't let the woman go. She took a step forward, reaching out her hand, and opened her mouth to call out. With a sick feeling, her world tilted, and moved away. The ground rose up to meet her, and Joel pulled her back by the hand.

"Are you alright?" He had her by the elbow, like she was an old lady, and his face was creased with concern. "Hazel?"

"Yeah," she said, blinking her eyes a few times.

"What's the matter? You walked onto the road." She looked, and the harsh straight lines of the street was there again. She was standing right on the kerb. A car pulled in to park right beside her and the engine noise grated painfully. She longed for the quiet of that dream again.

"Did I?" She shook her head.

"Come on, let's go sit down."

"It was beautiful," she said, but although the freshness and peace of the scene appealed to her, she also came out in tiny goosebumps when she thought about it.

"Hazel, you're scaring me." Joel rubbed his hands over the tops of her arms. She was scaring herself too, but this felt like something big, something important.

"Let's go this way," she said. They crossed the road and walked along the path. When she got to the Robert Burns statue, she reached up and ran her hand over the black stone, as much to feel that *she* was real as that the statue was solid and unmoving, constant as a rock.

It all looked so normal. The statue looked out over the Octagon from its platform, with intricate lamp posts and tall trees all around. Below were the covered walkways and beyond them, the bars and shops. Turning around, she saw the art gallery and a tall glass and concrete building. She felt breathless.

When she had seen it last, the statue stood out on a lonely grass hillside. It could have been the same place in another time, perhaps.

"You look like you're fading, Red," Joel said, holding her hand firmly as they waited to cross. "We'll get something hot into you. A feed always makes me feel better."

Hazel felt insubstantial and as light as a leaf on the wind. "Yeah. Food. Food is good."

CHAPTER THREE

*J*oel had reluctantly agreed to Hazel's protestations that she didn't need to see a doctor, but he was forceful about getting some food into her immediately. He sat next to her on the bench seat instead of facing her.

When he was ordering their burgers, Hazel sent a quick message to Briar, and she arrived just as they finished their meal. Her aunt would know what to do, Hazel was sure.

Briar patted the blue and green scarf she had wrapped around her head. She was wearing a long purple sweater over culottes.

"I've still got wet hair from my shower," she said. "I popped straight down the hill when I got your text. I'll get you both coffees. What do you want?"

"Something sweet and strong for both of us," Hazel said, looking at Joel for agreement. "Do you think they'll do an Irish coffee here?"

Briar raised one brow. "I can ask."

"Oh, and get Joel's one to take away." she said, ignoring the 'hey' that came from him.

"Getting rid of me?" Joel asked, turning to her and wrapping his arms around her, while Briar went up to the counter. "Are you sure you're going to be alright?"

"Yes," she said firmly. "I'm fine now with a bit of food in my belly." She looked over the mostly empty plates in front of them and laughed. "Okay fine, a lot of food. That was a big burger."

"I'm just looking after you."

"And I love it," she said, gently. "I need to chat with Briar, though. I think it's all coven-related and she'll be able to help."

"Ok, well, I'll see you soon," he said, sternly. "And when you get there, I'm going to look after you the hardest anyone has ever been looked after."

Hazel laughed. "Sounds good."

Briar came over with the takeaway coffee in a tall cup and passed it to Joel. "Here you go."

"Cheers," he said, leaning over to brush Hazel's forehead with the lightest of kisses as he stood up. "I'll leave you two ladies to it."

"He seems like a really nice guy," said Briar. "I'm happy that you two are still together."

"He is," Hazel said. She took a breath. "I know you must be dying to know what happened."

"All I got was a text message from my niece saying to meet you here. I am a little curious, yes. I was just getting out of the shower after a yoga class at the gym. So I dropped Moira off at home and came straight here."

"I'm sorry to interrupt your day," Hazel said.

Briar waved her hands, disregarding the interruption. "Coven stuff is always going to be important."

Hazel nodded. "It doesn't mean it's not annoying when it intrudes on the rest of your life. Anyway, I think

you'll want to hear this. I had a waking dream, or
vision— "

"Here you are." The waiter was young, and Hazel thought
he must be about twenty. "One hot chocolate with double
cream," he said, pushing the drink across the table. "One
Irish coffee with whiskey. And one caramel muffin. Would
you like anything else?"

"No thanks," Briar said. "This is plenty."

The waiter stood there, silent. When he finally turned
away, Hazel caught Briar's eye and they both collapsed into
laughter, trying to keep it quiet.

While the waiter was standing there, his mind was
spinning: What's the story with these two? Are they mother
and daughter or friends from work? Are they a couple?

"D. None of the above," Hazel whispered. "Nosy git."

Briar wiped her eyes. "Alright, I'd love to hear about this
vision." She dug her fork into the icing of the muffin and
lifted up a slice, admiring the fluffiness of the cake and the
caramel glaze, like the kitchen witch she was. "Those little
murmurs of magic should never be ignored. Neither should
dreams, and the prickle of intuition."

"No, they shouldn't," Hazel agreed. She floated the cream
around gently with a long spoon, letting the coffee smell
wash over her, bringing her back to the present, tethering her
to the ground. To the here and now.

"It happened in the Octagon," she said, and outlined the
vision for her aunt. "At the end of it, I saw a person... in a
brown... cloak... who I wanted to follow. They hurried down
the hill and out of sight... "

Briar looked up sharply from stirring her drink.

"A woman." Hazel glanced quickly at Briar as she said the
words at the same time. She felt that melancholy, that sense
that she had missed something again.

"Yes."

"I've had the same vision, I think," Briar said, staring off into the distance. "I didn't see it that clearly, but I remember the feeling of that hillside and the total peace, until I noticed the woman. So you felt you had to follow her?"

"Yes." When Hazel had been initiated as the Secret Keeper of their coven, Briar had told her that strange feelings of recognition might happen as she was learning to use her new powers. "Do you think it was déjà vu, like you warned me about?"

Her aunt nodded. "Remember how I told you that all the information has been given to you, but you need to get it out? Some think that when people have déjà vu, it is because they are seeing a bit of one of their previous lives. They have forgotten it but it lives on in their subconscious mind," she said, spreading her hands out on the table.

"But it's not our previous lives. Instead it's the lives of those witches in our family who came before us. We have been given the information. It's in there," she said, tapping her head, "but we're not aware of it. Until we can teach ourselves to access it. It comes in a strong feeling of recognition, or a vision, and it is often very disconcerting. It can be a shock the first few times."

Hazel nodded. "I was frightened, but also kind of wanted to know more." She was leaning forward now, keen to learn about it. She fiddled with the locket that she always wore, the amulet that was the link to her ancestors. "It sounds like that experiment with the coffee, where the students were asked to hold something for the lab assistant."

"Nope. Haven't heard of it," Briar said, shrugging. She absentmindedly swept the crumbs into a little pile.

"Well, basically, these university students didn't know anything about him beforehand. Then, during the experiment, the lab assistant asked the students to give him a hand as he went through a door."

"Okay."

"Then later the students had to rate his personality. If the university student had to hold a hot cup of coffee for the guy, they later rated him as warm and nice. If it was an iced coffee, they were far more likely to rate him as a cold and uncaring person. That was all it took. So their brains had been primed with subconscious information about the man which then affected their later actions. Hadley told me about it," she finished.

"Git," Briar said under her breath, which was almost like a reflex at this point, whenever Hadley's name was mentioned.

Hazel had to concede. "He wasn't too bad, really. He just wasn't for me. Anyway, it sounds like it works in a similar way. Unlocking something that is already in your subconscious."

"I think it does," Briar said, draining her cup. "I was never taught any of that, though. My teachings were all souls, herbs and moonshine. A mixture of both methods is probably about right. Can you think of something that might have triggered it for you?"

She shrugged. "The cathedral? Or maybe one of the people I saw," she said, thinking of Kirsten and Christo. So what should I expect next? More memories?" A shiver passed down Hazel's spine as she thought of the woman in the field. Would visions creep into her waking hours?

"I'm not sure." Briar rubbed her fingers across her forehead, smoothing away the lines, and Hazel remembered that her aunt was going through a rough time too, having lost some of her powers when she passed on the role of Secret Keeper to Hazel. "But I know one thing. Because you have had that vision, we need to get started with your training. We've got a lot of work to do."

That evening, Joel ran her a bath and made her a cup of camomile tea. He tucked her into bed early, smoothing her hair off her face.

"Did you learn anything useful from your aunt?"

"I think so," she said, grateful that he didn't probe any further. Hazel wasn't sure, yet, what the vision meant.

She slept well, as if the mental exhaustion of the day had tired her out as much as a good walk. When she woke, she read her book in bed for a few hours, then grew restless.

Gardening didn't wait for anyone, and the weeds had started curling up between the slats in the wooden verandah. She flicked nettles and foxgloves into a pile on the path, to be replanted somewhere else in the garden, where they wouldn't be in people's way. Every plant had its use. It was hard to think of anything else with her hands in the soil and the hum of growing plants all around.

But the energy felt *wrong*, somehow, she thought. She walked down the hill and trailed her fingers through the leaves, listening to the living core of them beneath the ground. One of the saplings had a black powder on the leaves and Hazel poured her magic into it, healing the leaf mould. There, that would do.

When she had nothing else to distract her, she opened her work laptop. She sat on the floor, papers spread all around her. Scattered amongst them were glossy articles ripped from magazines with pictures of Edinburgh or Adelaide. She had highlighted words like 'unique' and 'tropical".

Where is your mate today? Bonnie asked, as she loped into the room.

"He's allowed to go out by himself," she said, more

defensively than she meant to. "Meanwhile, I'm spending my Sunday coming up with promotional slogans," she muttered.

You love it, the dog said easily, moving to snuggle in next to Hazel's leg, crunching the papers as she shifted.

"Mm, yeah, I do," she admitted.

All of the Marketing Department were quietly working on the project around their other work, while pretending not to care too much. Hazel had laughed to herself as Perry desperately tried to look at the work she had done, offering her a new box of pens as an excuse. It was a pity advertising was all about being original. The new angle on the story.

The afternoon passed quickly, and soon enough, Hazel heard footsteps on the front verandah.

Bonnie lifted her head lazily as the door opened but dropped it back down, apparently satisfied that it was someone safe.

"Red?" Joel came in, smiling, carrying a pre-cooked chicken and some french bread. "I brought food. Is this you taking it easy?"

Hazel got up and followed him into the kitchen. "Lifesaver," she said, and her stomach grumbled loudly to underline her comment. "I've forgotten to eat all afternoon."

"You'll have to hang on, as this needs to be heated up." He switched on the oven. "Do you have salad ingredients?"

She nodded, and went to the fridge, pulling things out and carrying them over to the bench. She washed the lettuce and arranged it in a bowl with grated carrot, parsley and cherry tomatoes.

"I heard back from the bank," he said, dodging one of the hanging bunches of rosemary and sage. He sat on the stool next to where she was standing, and put his hand on her back. She leaned into him, and his light scent of wood and grass mixed with the fresh scent of herbs.

"What did they say?"

"Because of how 'inconsistent' my income is – that's the word they used – they want something as security or collateral. They aren't interested in my car."

"Really?" Hazel asked, keeping her lips pressed together so she didn't make any remarks about how old it was, and how hard it would be to find parts if the car needed repairs.

"The guy came out this afternoon. He had the papers all ready. He said they were thinking of using the cabin as security."

Hazel nodded. That made sense. She poured a little dressing over the salad, and tossed it with salad servers, before arranging avocado slices on top.

Joel sidled past her and put the roasting dish in the oven. "He had a good look around. I mean, he was probably there for an hour. Talked a lot about the state of the housing market. He thinks I should build more of the tiny houses and sell them."

"That's not a bad idea?"

He pushed one of the hanging bunches of herbs out of the way and it swung back and hit him in the face. "No, but then he saw the leak patch and completely changed his tune."

Hazel cringed. "Ah... shit." She hadn't had a chance to clear that up.

Joel was eyeing up the bunch of herbs as if it had a mind of its own. "He rang back then and said the only way he could do the loan is if I sell the house so that I've got a deposit. Reckons I'd get about fifteen thousand for it."

Hazel considered for a moment. It was a big deal for him to sell the cabin, especially after having to sell the family land so recently. He had built the cabin himself. It was his dream tiny house, and his last connection to his parents. And she could tell he was anxious about dealing with banks.

She tapped her fingers on the bench. She could have sworn she saw something tiny scuttle along the floor at the edge of her vision. What was it? Now that she thought of it, that feeling was familiar. Did she have white-tailed spiders in the house?

She bent down to have a look where the wooden floor met the wall. Nothing was there, but a small crack showed where it could have escaped.

"Are you okay?"

"Yup." She straightened. "What are you going to do, then?"

"Well, there's another bank on my list to try." He paced to the other end of the kitchen, and stopped in the doorway, testing its strength with his fist. It was a subconscious habit of his when he was stressed. "I doubt anyone is going to approve me, though."

Hazel felt waves of sadness and hopelessness from him, anxiety and fear. She chewed her bottom lip, deciding whether to speak. "You could.... you could stay here. There's heaps of room."

"What do you mean?" He looked seriously confused for a minute, and Hazel's heart banged in her chest. Had she said something that far out of line? Oh Goddess, was she being too clingy?

"You know, you sell the cabin and get the money from that. Then move in with me. Just as a temporary measure, of course."

He was staring at her, face inscrutable. She looked away. "My aunt doesn't charge too much rent," she went on, "and we could pay half each. You might not even need to get a loan at all. You could get a little shed to do your woodworking in. I'm... just throwing ideas out there."

Say something, damn you. Hazel looked out the window at

the verandah, where the ginger cat that always hung around
was pushing up against the table leg, arching to scratch itself.

"Why would I want to move in here?"

"I— "

"With you?"

"Forget it."

"You'd only be keeping me awake every night. I'd never get
any sleep."

She looked up. The edge of his mouth was twitching. He
was messing with her. She reached over to punch him in the
arm, but he moved out of the way.

He grinned, and dodged as she chased him around the
room. He pulled down a pan from its hook and held it up
between them.

"I think you want someone to cook for you," he said.

"You're lucky that's in the way."

"And fix things up for you."

She stared at him, hands on hips, eyes narrowed.

"What?"

"Oh, I'm trying to remember my nastiest hexes," she said.
"That's all. A spell to swell your nose, perhaps?"

"You wouldn't dare," he said, moving the pan out of the
way, and placing it on the bench. Never turning his back on
her though, she noted. He spread his hands, showing he
was vulnerable, stepped in close, and put his lips to her
neck. As he spoke, it tickled the spot just above her
collarbone.

"It's a plan," he said, one hand resting in the small of her
back and the other tucking her hair out of the way. "I like it."

"You're going to sell your house? Are you sure?"

"Mm hmm." His lips moved around her neck as he
planted kisses under her jaw, his stubble scratching a little. "I
can always build another cabin."

Hazel pulled back to look into his face. What he was saying didn't quite go with his emotions.

"As soon as the cabin sells, I'll be your resident non-witch advisor, if you'll have me. Just until I can get another one built. I'd love to move in with you."

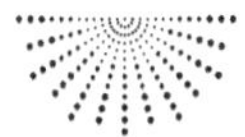

CHAPTER FOUR

Hazel trailed into the meeting room behind June, nursing her coffee. Monday mornings were bad enough without mysterious staffing meetings. Mysterious staffing meetings in unheated rooms? Well, that was torture.

"I hope they hurry up, I've got some more work to do on the city promotion project. How about you? Are you all ready?"

"I guess so," June said.

Hazel took a sip of her coffee and wrinkled her nose. Bitter. It seemed like someone was always changing suppliers around here. Even if it saved a few cents, it wasn't a good deal if it tasted less like coffee than the leftover sludge from an oil change. She gulped at the sludge, needing the pick-me-up. At least it was hot.

June fiddled with her cell phone. "It just feels like there is so much at stake. You don't want to end up with something embarrassing," she said. "Then you'll be famous for all the wrong reasons. You'll end up in a meme."

"Oh no, you're totally right," Hazel said, heart sinking as she remembered how people always made fun of town slogans. Particularly small towns in New Zealand that didn't have a lot going on.

She sat down at the table, pulling her jacket around her. The meeting room was freezing since the heating wasn't working properly. Hazel wriggled her toes inside her shoes to get the feeling back to them, and wrapped her hands around her mug.

June sighed. "My daughter is going to look at a flat today. Wish me luck."

"I wish you all the luck," Hazel said, sincerely. She crossed her fingers under the desk, and made a mental note to send a luck blessing to June tonight. Her daughter was almost as old as Hazel herself, and had come back to live at home, when June was starting a new relationship. Hazel hoped that June's daughter found a rental that she could afford, and that she could pay the bond. At fifty, June needed her space.

"Hey, are they hiring a new Admin person?" Hazel asked June in a quiet voice.

"I don't know, love. Normally, you know what's going on—"

Sia bustled in, looking harassed, and stood awkwardly near the door, smoothing down the front of her dress. Christo followed her in, silently counting heads. There were about ten of them in the meeting room, which was obviously enough, as he cleared his throat.

"Okay," he said. "I'm going to start by saying thank you for taking time out for this meeting. I know we're all busy."

People shuffled a little. It wasn't like Christo to notice if anyone was busy. It seemed like they were being buttered up for some bad news.

"We're still attracting people to the region, and our latest survey has shown that people are pretty happy. Not ecstatic, but we are doing okay," he said, then he paused, and licked his lips. Hazel felt a little nervousness coming from him.

"Let's take our game to another level," he said. "We want to bring in some fresh perspective to the team, so we are reviewing the future shape of the business. We're looking for creativity and efficiency. We are going to have the absolute best people leading the change management."

People looked at each other, uneasy. What was he talking about? Was he going to bring in one of his mates to the team?

Get on with it, Hazel thought.

"So I'm going to leave off here, and let our new Marketing Strategy Manager introduce herself."

New Marketing Strategy Manager! Hazel looked across at Sia. She was wearing a bright green dress today, with her dark hair done in a lovely French roll. Her boss worked the hardest of them all. And they were bringing in someone new to slot in right above her.

Hazel looked around, as a woman stepped out to the front. She must have slipped in while Christo was talking. She put her fingertips lightly on the table, and leaned forward.

That blonde bob. That small stature. That tiny, perfect nose. Hazel went hot all over as several of her worlds collided at the same time.

"I'm Kirsten Treleaven," she said, in her calm voice, which took Hazel straight back to the night in Joel's garden – the sound of that voice boring into her mind, telling her that she was in pain, the lack of control she had over the situation, the spine-chilling fear.

This was the woman that had arranged for Joel's house to be sold, the one who had blackmailed Mandy. She was going to be Hazel's boss? June elbowed her and she looked down, realizing that she had clutched on to June's arm. She relaxed her grip and rubbed her hands over her arms to warm them.

Kirsten smoothed her navy skirt. "I've done so many things, which I believe will help me to help you. I've had experience as the CEO of a successful start-up company and I'm also a Manager in the cosmetic industry space."

A beauty salon. Hazel remembered with shame how she had waltzed into Brows. Her blood seemed to be running cold, and her feet felt like ice blocks.

"I've won awards for my environmental work many years ago. Of course, I've known Christo for a long time." She smiled over at him. "Some of you I have already met, as well." Kirsten met Hazel's eyes.

"Great," Christo said. "Kirsten will be taking the strategy meeting next Thursday. Until then, let's make her feel welcome. Thanks, team."

Hazel stood up, a smile painted onto her face. As she passed Sia, she sensed her boss wondering why she had been passed over for promotion, and ashamed about what her team must think, but determined to prove herself. Sia's arms were crossed and she looked as if she was trying as hard as Hazel to keep the smile on.

Hazel walked out of the room, out of the front doors and somehow found herself at the coffee shop round the corner. The stuffy heat was welcome. She sank into the velvet booth seat and tucked into a boysenberry tart with careless abandon.

This was bad. This was very bad.

"Hazel? Any ideas?" Sia's heels clicked over the wooden floor in the conference room. Hazel felt suddenly sick, thinking that her boss never had a chance of promotion. It was all planned out.

"Hmm." She had plenty of things to say, mostly involving a certain woman, but none were appropriate to share with the group.

"Just broad themes to start with, please. This is a casual brainstorming session. Remember, we'll choose a few of you to go into the next round."

Her boss passed Hazel the whiteboard marker. She took it, but twirled it absently around. A city tagline was such a hard thing to get right. "I think it's going to be tough to come up with something that everyone agrees on. I mean, what is Dunedin all about? Surely everyone likes something different about it. Why don't we ask the public to come up with a new tagline? Have a competition in the paper?"

"Yes, I second that," Perry Strachan said, fiddling with his phone, which caught the light and shone in Hazel's eyes.

"That has worked in the past, but I don't think so this time," Sia said. "I had a phone call from Christo himself. It has to be done by the middle of next month. We just don't have the time."

Hazel sighed, and watched as her boss slumped into a chair.

They are desperate to look good. And it's our job to make them look good, Sia thought.

Hazel wrote 'heritage', 'arts' and 'welcoming'. She passed the pen on to June, who wrote something in her characteristic messy cursive.

"What does that say?" Hazel joked.

June gave her a tight-lipped look. "Nature's playground," she said. *That one kept me up all night. I really need this. It's hard enough dating at my age, let alone with these apps! I need to have the house to myself.*

Hazel looked at her with sympathy. She knew June was desperate for the bonus, as she was going to pay her daughter's bond on the new rental property. Hazel decided then that if she won the bonus, she'd give half of the money to her friend. And the other half to Joel.

After a few more minutes, Sia stood up and circled some of the words. "Okay, I think we'll focus on two of those and come up with as many as we can. Nature and welcoming. Get your idea boards ready for the next meeting."

"When will it be?" Hazel asked.

"That's the one on Thursday," Sia said. *If I had to guess. Nobody tells me anything around here. Found out at the same time as everyone else that I didn't get the job.*

Hazel reached out a hand to her, but didn't know what to say, since she wasn't supposed to know that Sia had applied.

Her boss looked up. "And don't forget about the baby photo contest tomorrow."

A chorus of groans accompanied this statement, and they filed out. "The photos are all stored away," June complained.

Sia was packing up her things, and Hazel took her time straightening the chairs, waiting until everyone had left.

"You are a really great boss," Hazel said, wanting to give her boss something. "You've taught me so much and I can see how hard you work."

"Well, thanks," Sia said, surprised, then laughed. "Don't think that flattery will get you any further in the competition, though."

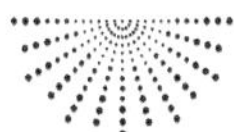

CHAPTER FIVE

*H*azel tossed and turned all night, thinking of the new strategy manager. Kirsten's face streamed across her vision, watching her every move. Standing behind her desk. Looking up her employee files. That powerful voice telling her what to do.

Hazel often played things out, thinking of all possible endings, but she had never once considered this. Of all the people to come in as the new boss, this was the absolute worst scenario.

She slapped at her phone to check the time. 4:51.

When the first light started coming in the window, she finally gave in and got up, wrapping her dressing gown around her. Bonnie padded along after her into the kitchen.

On the rare times when Hazel was up early, she loved this time of day. She flicked the jug on and sat on the chair with a book, watching the first rays of light reaching over the garden and alighting on the dew-covered plants, and listening to the first chirrups of the birds in the valley.

She skimmed the same page for the third time, as her mind wandered back to the office. The more she pondered, the more it seemed that it wasn't a coincidence. She had no qualms about saying that Kirsten had been employed for a reason. It wasn't to help the company, she was sure. Hazel would even go so far as to say it was to keep an eye on her.

Should she call in sick today? It was tempting.

She could spend the morning reading on the verandah, wrapped in a blanket, listening to the birdsong.

Afterwards, she could pack a picnic and Joel and her could eat it in the dinghy at the bottom of his garden. She thought of the last picnic they had shared, where they fed each other grapes and strawberries dipped in chocolate.

No, she thought, mentally slapping herself in the face. She would have to face up to Kirsten at some point.

It wouldn't be easy, working with someone she didn't trust. But knowing that Kirsten was nearby could be useful. Keep your friends close and your enemies closer, wasn't that the saying? Hazel could make it work to her advantage, she was sure.

***

"There." Hazel picked up her moisturisers, cleansers and make up remover, and placed them in the drawer. Joel's toiletries would fit on that shelf nicely. She wiped around the basin with her cloth, pausing to look at herself in the mirror. Her hair was pulled into a messy red bun on top of her head.

"Hmmm," she said into the mirror. The long purple t-shirt Hazel wore to bed was looking a bit faded. Oh well. It was comfortable. He would see her in all her period pants, ancient holey pyjamas and muffin-top-crushing glory soon enough.

She wandered out into the lounge, where Bonnie was lying in the middle of absolute carnage. The buyer was going to pick up the cabin in the morning. Joel's bed leaned against the wall, and boxes, rugs and chests of drawers almost covered the floor. A few newly made chests stood in the hallway, and the smell of oiled wood drifted to her.

It's lucky he only has a tiny house, she thought. *Imagine how much stuff there would be otherwise.*

It had taken a few days for the cabin to sell, and Joel was surrounded by a cloud of sadness as he cleared it out, throwing out old magazines and bringing boxes over. She honestly had no idea where he kept it all. It reminded her of those magical bags that are bigger on the inside than the outside.

Hazel felt for him, but she had enough to worry about with work. Whispers flew over coffee cups in the break room, and people bent their heads together, murmuring quietly. Rumours were tossed back and forth that a restructure was coming. Just today, Hazel had walked into Sia's office when she was on the phone, and her boss had quickly stopped mid-sentence, guilt and anger radiating from her.

Perry was almost running between the break room and the supplies room, probing anyone that unknowingly entered either room for a scrap of information. He was deathly afraid that he would be getting the chop.

"No thinking about work," she told herself now, firmly. "We need a moving in feast."

She pulled out some salami, grapes and Brie cheese from the fridge. Next, she opened a packet of crackers, fanning them out at the edge. She placed a ramekin of hummus in the middle with a flourish.

Maybe it's a little over the top, she thought. But she didn't care. Joel would appreciate it. He was always hungry.

It's about the best he'll get from you in the kitchen. You'll get his hopes up. Then when you pull out the two minute noodles and the frozen pies, they'll come crashing down.

Hazel glared at the dog. "You be quiet," she said. "Otherwise you'll be getting tinned dog food for dinner."

I've never worked with a witch who can't cook before.

"I can cook. I just choose not to."

A snort came from near ground level.

She took the platter out to the lounge and cleared a path through the boxes so she could see the tv from the couch. Bonnie flopped down next to her on the floor, nose twitching at the cheese.

She flicked the television to her favourite show. Would Joel want to watch this with her? For that matter, did he watch the news each night? How often did he wash his sheets? There were so many things they still didn't know about each other. But they'd find out all those things, for better or worse.

Hazel stretched out, listening to the whirr of the heater, and soon drifted off to sleep.

She woke up much later, hair stuck to her face. The television was bright against the darkness, still blaring even though nobody was listening. The room was stuffy. She had half a cracker in her hand, and the remainder of the cheese on the tray was looking a bit past it. She threw it to Bonnie, who caught it neatly.

What time was it? She checked her phone. 11:39. *Don't text in anger*, she thought, hesitating with her finger over the send button.

Turning off the television and the heater, she headed off to bed, alone. A spiky question prickled at the back of her thoughts. Had he changed his mind?

"Where did you get to last night?" Hazel asked, when Joel turned up at her door as she was putting her jacket on to go to work. He was carrying a small bag of clothes. His hair was messier than usual, and he had shadows under his eyes.

"Something came up, but I've sorted it." He marched inside, put the bag down, and headed for the door.

Hazel looked around the room. She had long since cleaned up the platter from last night, tipping the crackers carefully into a biscuit tin and sliding the salami into the rubbish bin. She had eaten grapes that were browning at one end, popping them resentfully off their stems, and vacuumed the floor around the coffee table. Usually she cleaned up with magic, but sometimes hoovering was good for the soul.

It's probably nothing, Bonnie sent to her. *He's a good one. You know that.*

"Don't dogs just love everyone?" she whispered.

No way! We can sense cat people a mile off.

Hazel stopped chewing her fingernail, shook off the thoughts and followed him outside, catching up when he was doing his shoelace on the path.

"Are you sure you're alright?" Hazel sensed shame and guilt from him, and wondered what could possibly have gone on. She followed him towards his gate, itching to reach out with her thoughts...

"Yeah, I am good now." He paused to open the gate and gave her a quick peck on the cheek. "Everything is going to be just fine."

"Where... where did you sleep?" she asked, thinking of his bed on its side in her lounge, safely packed in a sheet of plastic.

"Oh, I crashed at my cousin's place. He asked me to watch the rugby with him on Saturday night if you want to come?"

"Ah," she said, letting out a breath. His cousin. Scott. Hazel picked her way past, not looking at him.

The cabin was standing with its door open, like a sad and bewildered guest that has been unceremoniously dismissed. One cupboard door was hanging open. There was nothing inside, and all of the furniture had been folded away neatly. She walked in, her footsteps hollow.

She felt a presence behind her. "The old place is looking a bit sad, isn't she?" he asked, in a low voice. "I'll move in to your place this afternoon, okay?"

"I was waiting for you last night." Her voice came out reproachful, almost whiny. She hated the way it sounded. Why couldn't he simply tell her where he'd been?

"I — "

She made up her mind. If he waited two more seconds, she would reach into his mind. Find out where he was last night. Find out why he felt guilty. Was it just for selling the cabin? Did he feel like he had betrayed his parents' memory?

A roaring engine noise came from the street, and Joel wiped his hands on his jeans. "Shit, sorry. Sounds like the truck. This is it, I guess."

Hazel breathed out, and walked off, fists clenched, before she did something that might hurt them both.

At work, June was at the office before her for once. Hazel hung up her coat on the hook.

"There you are," June said, handing Hazel her reusable coffee cup.

"Good service," Hazel said, and smiled at her friend, grateful that she didn't have to brave the office coffee.

"Double mocha latte with cream. No sugar," June said. "Hope it's not too cold. They were ready at 8:25."

"Oh haha," Hazel said. She looked at the clock, which read 8:32. "Very funny. I'm sure it will be delicious."

"Have you put your photo up?" she asked Hazel, gesturing to the pinboard at the far end of the open-plan office.

"Not yet," she replied. As well as being a strange relic that no longer made sense in the digital age, office baby photo competitions had always been embarrassing for Hazel. She got a strong sense of who each person was just from the photo and often guessed right, even when the baby picture looked nothing like the adult. To make up for it, she had to close her eyes when she guessed, so she got some wrong.

She waited until nobody else was near the noticeboard, then reached into her handbag to get her photo. Dark red hair and a pointy chin. Pretty obvious to anyone, really.

She walked over to the noticeboard and stuck a pin in her photo next to the number 18. Most of the photos were in the muted colours of the '70's and '80's. There was Perry, who was a baby holding onto his mother's leg and a softly-spoken private school boy from Hamilton who struggled to be listened to. The bald one with the bow headband who radiated a love for travel and cats, that was June. If the baby with the smile that almost split her face in half wasn't Sia, Hazel would eat her witch hat. That love for family was recognizable anywhere.

And this one. A face framed with curls. Hazel reeled back from the wall as the office disappeared and dark clouds closed in on the edges of her vision. Everything went dark.

Not now, she thought, desperately. Her heart raced. She couldn't see. As she waved her hands around to get a grasp on *something*, her senses sharpened. She could smell a faint scent of horse. A dog barked far away.

As her eyes got used to the dark, she realized she was standing very close to a wooden building. She backed up until something butted into the back of her thighs.

"Not that ugly, are they?" Perry said. The bright room came back, the desk behind her, the carpet beneath her feet. She squinted her eyes.

"What? The babies? No, no, they're very bright... Cute! I mean, cute. I just... thought standing back further might give me a better perspective."

She walked back to her desk, and practiced some deep breathing behind her computer screen.

'Keep calm and carry sage' was what her grannie Em would say. Next, she had to run a meeting between an angry ratepayer and the person who organised the fireworks event right next door to his house. There would be enough sparks in the conference room, she thought.

She sent a message to Briar. "It happened again."

Almost instantly, she got a message back from her aunt. "First lesson tomorrow. Bring an open mind. Meet you at the gardens after work."

CHAPTER SIX

Hazel moved her head from side to side, stretching the aching muscles down the sides of her neck, then blew out her breath in a long puff. A freezing wind blew through the trees in the botanical gardens. It wasn't July yet, but it already felt like the depths of winter. It was all she could do not to stomp her foot.

"Work is horrible at the moment," she said.

"Tell me about it later, love," Briar said. "There's always going to be bad days. Now be patient. It's like what you've done in the past, but different."

Hazel closed her eyes. "That's helpful," she said drily. All her muscles were seizing up in the cold, as she concentrated all her energy on her mind's eye. She shook out her shoulders.

"I mean the meditation you go through, when you work with your psychic powers. It's not too different to that. Clear the mind."

Briar's lashes flicked down, so she was staring at the flower bed beside her, face turned half away.

You have been given The Gift, her aunt's thoughts came to her. *But that is only one piece of the puzzle.*

Her aunt looked for all the world as if she was contemplating picking one of the rhododendrons growing beside them, but didn't really care enough to do so.

Hazel could hear her better now than if Briar spoke the words out loud. Inside their minds, there was no background noise, no wind, and each word was received at a volume that was clear and audible.

When you become the Secret Keeper, Briar thought, *you get the knowledge of our Ancestors, the Redferne family. You get to know where they came from, who they were, what they did and what they knew. But the knowledge can't go to just anybody.*

Hazel wished Briar would get on with it. Her aunt seemed to repeat all of this every time they worked together, almost religiously, like some sort of invocation.

She fingered the locket that would enable her to get the memories of their family. It was such a small and simple thing that was so important. It wasn't worth anything. Nobody would even look twice at it. She guessed that was the point of it.

You get all of this knowledge stuffed into your mind, but you won't know it, straight away. You have to learn to access it.

"It could take a long time until you can access the... information," Briar said out loud. "The hard drive," she added, louder, presumably in case anyone was listening.

"Okay, I'll try again." Hazel sat down again, cross-legged, on her jacket on the ground. Her mind wandered to Joel, who had officially moved in last night. He was awake before her this morning and brought her a coffee in bed.

"It will be worth it, Hazel," her aunt said. "Think of how many spells one witch would learn in a lifetime. And you'll have many lifetimes worth."

"Do you miss it?"

"Very much. But time goes on. Things change. Witches become crones."

Hazel nodded. Eyes closed, she watched the colours behind her eyelids bleed together and looked for the black dot, which was the key to her mind's eye.

"What do you see?" Briar asked under her breath, and waited.

Hazel teased it apart and squeezed herself through.

"I'm coming out of the tunnel. I'm on a bridge. It's not very wide. Everything is dark all around but I know it's a long, long way down. I am higher up than I've ever been in real life." She shuddered.

"Yes?"

"I step forward... and there's something there. I can't go any further."

"Keep walking."

But she couldn't. It was almost like walking the wrong way on an escalator. She imagined a thin, cold wind up around her ears, reaching into the back of her coat. To either side was the feeling of nothingness, just a dark, crawling horror that if she slipped she would fall. And she wouldn't stop falling.

"What does this have to do with— "

"Push through it, Hazel."

"I'm trying... but I can't see what I'm pushing against, so I don't even know how to get through. It changes shape so that it's always in front of me."

"If it's invisible, then let your mind give it shape. Bring it to life."

Hands out in front, Hazel pushed into the thing, which was a sort of dense wind. An amorphous blob. *Bring it to life*, she breathed. Okay then. And beneath her fingers, it changed, filling in the particles, solidifying. Her hands touched something fuzzy, cool and slimy. Hairy.

Hazel opened her eyes. Her palms were sweaty and she wiped them on her jeans.

"Hey, it's alright," Briar said. "It took me a year, I think."

"Yeah," she smiled weakly. She had definitely been watching too much horror lately. Why couldn't the thing have turned into Bradley Cooper? She'd be much more keen to do her exercises.

"I know you. You want to ace this first off, like it's some maths test." Briar grinned, and pulled her scarf up over her ears. "But it's too bloody freezing to do this any longer today. Do you want to come and get one of our chocolate brownies at the cafe?"

"I won't, today. Thanks." Hazel put her hand out, and Briar grabbed it and pulled her up. She thought she'd much rather have a large whiskey. All of this slipping into other states of consciousness was hard on the nerves.

"Alright, well, I've got to get back, love," Briar said, leaning in and kissing her on the cheek. "I'm practising for the barista awards. Moira thinks it will be good publicity for the cafe."

"You'll be great, Bry."

Her aunt grimaced. "I told her I'm too old for it. Most of the other entrants are in their twenties. They can dazzle the judges with their charm."

"Hey, you can charm the judges too. You know your coffees are the best."

"Maybe. Anyway, keep safe, Hazel." Briar stuffed her magazine into her bag and headed down the hill to her car.

Hazel caught the bus back through town for their first shop together as a couple. She was exhausted, but she wouldn't have missed this for anything.

She waited outside the supermarket, coat turned up against the wind. When she spotted Joel, she reached in for a hug. He smelled like her honey blossom and peach body wash.

"Hello, house mate," she said.

"Right, who's in charge?" he asked, pulling out a trolley from the row with a clacking sound.

"If you have to ask, it mustn't be you." Hazel laughed, and nudged him in the ribs. "No, you're the cook, so I don't mind."

Joel grabbed a few different meats, pausing to check if she was happy with them. He turned the lamb this way and that, and compared prices and contents of sausages.

"The ones that are mostly meat are the best," he said, placing them in the trolley. This seemed like his happy place. She could almost see him as a stone age hunter eyeing up his prey, comparing the animals lurking in the savannah, then returning, victorious, to lay down his spoils and present her with... a packet of sausages.

"Yeah, honestly, I usually eat soup but I'm happy with whatever."

"Just don't ask you to cook it, right?"

She nodded.

"Biscuits," he said, musing at the aisle filled with different coloured packets. Hazel reached for something chocolate oozing with caramel and dropped them in the trolley, at the same time as Joel added a packet of orange and sultana cookies. They looked at each other.

"We can get both." It filled her with happiness to do something so normal, so boring, with someone else. Nothing supernatural, or springing from the realms of darkness. A simple grocery shop. Usually, it was a brisk walk around the supermarket, with most of her time spent browsing the instant soup flavours. She slipped her arm around his waist.

They went home together in Joel's car, and unpacked the groceries in companiable silence.

"What would you like for tea? I can make pancakes?"

"Yeah, I guess," she said, doubtfully, reaching up to put the baked beans in the top of the pantry. "Why not?"

"We could eat cake and ice cream, with toffee sauce and a cherry on top, for dinner if we like," he said to her, a childish grin on his face. "We're adults."

"Yeah, we are. We're eating dinner at 8:30pm!"

Joel smiled. He added the flour, milk and eggs to the bowl and whipped it all up. When they started to bubble, he flipped them in the pan, catching them expertly.

Hazel started clearing up the ingredients he'd used and carefully grabbed the egg shells to store outside in a bucket.

"They're good for planting with tomatoes," she said, when she saw him watching. "Little things like that keep coming back to me from when I was young."

Bonnie wandered in and flopped down on the floor. Hazel got out the maple syrup and a ripe banana, and Joel flipped the pancakes onto the plates. They ate by candlelight, a bottle of wine between them on the table.

"Cheers," he said, lifting his glass.

"To pancake dinners."

CHAPTER SEVEN

The rest of the week passed in stress and worry at work, and domestic bliss in the stolen moments that Hazel spent with Joel.

On Saturday morning, Joel was up and out of the house long before Hazel woke. She got up, stretched and threw on jeans and an oversized jersey. The floorboards were freezing, and the house was quiet. Bonnie was nowhere to be seen.

She opened the screen door and looked outside, thinking of the view Joel had from the section next door. Soon enough, her thoughts moved to what drew people to the city. She supposed it wasn't too different to what drew people to Dunedin in the 19th century. The surroundings, the people and the promise of a better life.

The grass was frosted in silver, so she knew it would be a sunny afternoon. She looked out at the sweetpeas and red - were they poppies? - toadstools in the back yard. Toadstools? She stepped further out to look but her bare feet protested at the icy verandah underfoot. The bright red fungi popped up from the lawn, some as large as grapefruit. She would have to find a spell to get rid of them later on.

It wasn't until late afternoon that he came back, stopping to peck her on the cheek. He smelled of a new aftershave.

"I got the loan," he said, spreading his hands. "They rang this morning and I've just signed the papers."

"Oh, that is great news." Hazel wondered if that was why Scott said Joel would be fine now. Did he know someone in the bank and know the loan would be approved? In any case, it meant he could get on with making more wooden products to sell. And if Hazel got the bonus, she could give it to June. "And you got yourself a haircut," she said, admiringly. "You look very handsome."

His light brown hair was short at the sides and slightly longer at the top. His face was closely shaved, accentuating his jaw. He wore a light purple business shirt and dark pants.

"Where did you even get those clothes?" she asked.

"Scott and I went shopping," he said casually. He walked into the bedroom, unbuttoning the shirt. "I'm just going to get my rugby shirt on, then I'm off." His time at the gym had paid dividends, Hazel thought, appreciating the fine muscling around his shoulders. "Are you coming?"

She was surprised at his dismissive tone, almost as if he couldn't care less whether she joined him or not.

"Are you going to your cousin's place to watch?"

He slipped on a black rugby jersey. "No. Down to the pub."

"Um... Okay. I will." Hazel didn't like watching rugby, and the thought of a bar full of drunk people made her head hurt. But Scott Hills worked for the company that had bought Joel's property. His own cousin! And she couldn't help but wonder what made him tick.

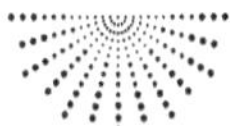

CHAPTER EIGHT

"It's warm in here," she said to Joel and Scott, but wasn't even sure if anyone heard her since it was so loud in the pub. She weaved her way around the people, ignoring the thoughts of one man who eyed her up as she sidled past. What was on his mind involved her in considerably less clothes than she was wearing now and a pint of Guinness.

Would you like it if I kicked you in the tender bits? she thought. *Or turned your hair instantly grey?*

"Yes," the man yelled, pumping his fist, and the rest of the pub joined him in cheering. She laughed to herself. It must have been a try.

Hazel shut the door thankfully in the cool of the corridor. She didn't usually come out to places like this, because of the maelstrom of noise and emotion. She was having trouble making out specific thoughts, among the enthusiasm and heart-pounding energy of the rugby fans. But the truth of the matter was that she was insanely curious about Joel's relationship with his cousin.

A long sigh escaped her as she looked into the bathroom mirror. Scott and Joel still seemed to be good friends, even after everything that had happened. But she wasn't going to be able to find out much from Scott like this. The longest sentence either of them had said tonight was 'Wedges or fries?'.

Hazel went back to the table and passed the time working on her powers, by picking one person from nearby and blocking out all the background thoughts and moods from the crowd. If she looked at that old man with the Scottish cap on and stared as hard as she could, she might be able to tune out everything else.

But a roar from the crowd put her off completely, as the player missed the conversion. She stared into her gin and tonic. She would gladly leave to find a quiet spot with a book.

As the evening wore on, the people in the bar became a bit more subdued as the score wasn't on their side. At half time, some left, or crept into the pokies room, riffling in their wallets.

Scott went to play a game of pool around the corner and came back to the table ten minutes later, flushed and waving his beer around. "Easy win," he said. "He only potted three. Do you want a game?" This was directed at Joel.

"What? Nah. This is getting exciting," he said, turning back towards the big screen.

"It's a lost cause, mate."

"I'll play," Hazel said. This was her chance.

She followed him over to the table and chose a cue, waiting while he set up the balls.

"You break. This shouldn't take too long." Scott got his phone out and placed it on the edge of the table.

Hazel looked at him, eyebrows raised and both hands

gripping her cue. How did he know if she was any good at pool or not?

She lined up her shot and hit the front ball straight in the middle. It hit with a clink, and the rest of the balls hardly scattered at all. *Alright, not a good start,* she said to herself, ignoring his smug look.

"You live next door to Joel?" he asked, walking around to line up his shot.

"Yeah, it's my aunt's place," she answered. "I haven't played this in ages."

Scott had his shot and sunk one ball, then another. Hazel couldn't help but be impressed. She racked her brains to figure out how to get him talking so that she could find out more about his role in the sale of his cousin's land.

"What do you do for a job?" She sidestepped around the table, waiting for the person at the next table to take their shot, before she got into position.

"I work for a property company. Been there almost a year. What about you?"

"I work for the council. What did you do before that?"

"Surveying. It was alright. Then I had about six months off." *I was made redundant, because I wouldn't take a sideways move, a position which would mean longer hours and more stress. I lost all my confidence.* The thoughts floated to her, but she couldn't make out the rest, as the tumultuous noise of the rugby fans came to her again.

"That's a bit of a change."

"I was actually head-hunted for this position that I've got now." *God, that sounds impressive saying it out loud,* he thought, and she cringed.

"That's pretty cool. I bet you're really busy." Okay, now she was getting somewhere. So Scott was shunted out of his previous job unfairly, and lost his nerve. He had spent a few months out of work. She wondered if Kirsten had offered him confidence in a bottle, along with the job.

"Yeah, we have a few developments happening right now on the edges of town. People moving here from Auckland or Wellington."

"Property prices are just insane," Hazel said. It simply wasn't achievable for most people to buy their first house now. "They keep saying this whole bubble is going to burst."

"Been saying that for thirty years," he said, dismissing her with a flick of the wrist.

Hazel looked at the table. She had three left, and he had two. She sent the white ball down the far end of the table, nudging hers close to the pocket.

"That was a push shot," he said, accusing. "Lose a turn. I get two turns."

Really? She rolled her eyes as he stepped up to the table.

Enough dancing around the issue. As he was about to have his next turn, she took a deep breath and asked, "What are you going to do with Joel's property? Will you develop it?"

He straightened, and looked at her, face inscrutable. "We're happy to sit on that one for a while, actually."

He took his turn and potted one of his balls. Now he only had one to go, as well as the black. He missed. He bit his lip to stop from swearing, and walked away from the table.

"Don't you feel bad about taking it from him? From your aunt and uncle?"

He looked up sharply. "It was a fair sale."

"Was it?" she asked, but quietly. He didn't seem to radiate any guilt, so Hazel wondered if he knew that it hadn't been entirely above board. She didn't push it. If he wasn't aware of the dodgy bank dealings leading to the mortgagee sale, there was no point blaming him. She sighed.

It was all such a huge mess. She remembered how Mandy had asked her to stop Kirsten from playing with other people's lives. Hazel wanted to help, she really did. But it felt insurmountable.

"I think things will be looking up for Joel from now on. He's got his shit sorted."

"Why do you say that?" Hazel lined up her shot and got the ball in the middle pocket, then took her time chalking up her cue.

"Well, it couldn't get much worse for him, right?" he sneered. "Gotta go up some time." He took a swig of his beer.

This guy was really something. Did he never doubt himself? Never think well of others?

"My turn again, isn't it?" she asked. The white travelled down the table, as if of its own accord, and her other ball was clunked into the pocket.

She heard a low whistle. Joel had come over and was holding up his beer in congratulations.

Hazel's heart beat fast as she looked over the table. Fortunately, she was set up right next to the black ball. She couldn't miss it or she would have lost the whole game. The white gently kissed the black and it rolled tantalizingly close to the pocket but didn't quite drop in. It gave Scott another chance.

"Lucky," Scott muttered. He had a difficult shot, from one end of the table to the other, but he hit the white hard, confidently. The white ricocheted down the table and hit his last ball in. Scott turned from the table but the white was headed towards the corner. It plunked into the black hard, and knocked them both into the pocket. Foul and forfeit.

For the rest of the rugby game, Scott had to buy the drinks. Hazel thought that was silly, but it was their long standing rule, so who was she to disagree?

"What would you like?" he asked under his breath, almost as if the words were being forced out of him. He obviously didn't lose at pool very often.

"Another of the same, thanks." She smiled brightly at him.

It was later in the car on the way home, that Joel turned to her, an admiring grin on his face. "You totally magicked that shot, right?"

They turned up the hill towards home, and Hazel got a little glow of happiness right around her ribcage that they were both going to the same place. "Yeah. I feel a little guilty, but he was being such a... " She trailed off, thinking of the perfect word.

"Douche?"

"Swinge-buckling coxcomb," she finally settled on. "As Shakespeare might say. It's typical that you turned up for the one shot where I used magic. All the rest I did myself."

The headlights of a car coming down the hill flashed over them. "He probably has you pegged as some sort of pool shark now." Joel glanced over at her. "Did you have a good time tonight?"

"It was fine, but it's not really my thing. I'll leave the rugby games to you in future."

Hazel tried to imagine what it would have been like for Joel growing up with his cousin. Everything a competition. She could see why Joel often felt like he wasn't successful, when Scott never shut up about how great he was.

The evening wasn't entirely wasted, since she learnt more about his cousin, Hazel reflected. As always though, every little piece of the puzzle threw up more questions than answers.

Joel reached over and rubbed his fingers along the back of her neck.

"I suppose you're alright at pool, Red," he said, "but your insult game could use some work."

CHAPTER NINE

She took the bus down the hill on Sunday morning to meet Briar again. She looked up the history of The Exchange square and scrolled past images until she found one that looked very like what she had seen. It was a black and white of the Dunedin Exchange building and post office. The picture was from 1885. Hazel let out a gasp. It was one thing to think she was seeing the past, but another to know she had actually been there. Been *then*.

A new excitement spurred her on, as she climbed up the hill to where Briar was waiting.

"Hi, sweetie, I brought you something from the cafe. One for you and one for Joel." Hazel opened the box and reached in to take one of the cupcakes. It was at least twice the size of a normal cupcake. She tasted raspberry and crunched through a chunk of white chocolate.

"Mmm. Amazing," she said, dipping a finger into the icing. "This is my breakfast."

"It has a little something for concentration in it, too." her aunt said, raising her eyebrows at Hazel.

"Okay, I get it," she said, wiping the crumbs off her lap. "I'll get started."

Hazel was up on the bridge and the keening, cold wind blew around her ears, reaching into the back of her coat. She made herself peek over the side and immediately wished she hadn't, as the blackness threatened to pull her in.

Hazel opened one eye to check Briar was still there with her. Her aunt nodded reassuringly, the winter sun behind her. The blackness was only in her mind.

Breathing into her centre, Hazel returned to the bridge. She steadied herself, taking two deep breaths. In and out.

"Follow what scares you," Briar said.

This time, because she had taken one step, she knew she could take another. She turned side on, lifted her head and gritted her teeth, thinking of what was coming.

"This is part of becoming an elder witch, Hazel. You'll be able to help the younger witches that come through the coven."

She nodded, and made herself shuffle forward, although sweat dripped down between her breasts and her legs were jelly. Ahead was the shapeless gas. It solidified as she stepped towards it and she put her hands out, bringing it to life with her mind.

Bring it to life. Follow what scares you.

She remembered the woman from the vision, thinking of how she had felt a longing to know more but also a nameless fear.

Say the alphabet backwards.

Hazel ignored that one, concentrating on what was in front of her. How do you bring it to life? What would an artist do if they were painting a portrait?

She pictured the woman as well as she could, painting the details in her mind, the cloak, the crook of her back, the fingers that were never still, the way the hood cast shadows on her face.

She moved forward. The space next to her filled with places, meadows, roads and rooms in little wooden buildings. Hazel dared to look over the side of the bridge again, painting in the details. People floated in the air; old, young, men, women, two children and a cherubic-faced baby. It seemed like these were all the people the woman had known.

And just like that, she got it. Her blood pulsed through her veins. Being the Secret Keeper meant memories were given to her. It was like hearing the thoughts of her dead ancestors.

Oh, bloody hell, it was perfect! In her job, she had to think about things from the point of view of her audience. What did they like? How did they talk? Where did they go and what did they do? What were their greatest fears and dreams? It was easy for someone like her who could hear other people's thoughts. But what we think doesn't exist in a vacuum.

A psychic witch was perfect for this. It wasn't enough just to see the memories. She had to understand the person, as if looking at a whole piece of art, woven through with threads of their culture and community, their past and future.

"I think I'm finally starting to understand," she said, opening her eyes.

She had to find out who the woman was.

It was clearer in her mind now. Things didn't just happen. Nothing was coincidence, wasn't that what she had always been taught? Something had triggered that vision.

The quicker she found out what it was, the quicker she could get back to living a quiet life with Joel. Evenings with laughter and kisses, pancakes and wine and roaring fires.

She put on her coat and biked to the Octagon. By the time

she got there, her hands were freezing and it was dark outside the pools of light from the streetlamps. She had to blow on her fingers to warm them up.

A couple walked along, holding hands. Another man smoked outside a restaurant, his jacket hood pulled up.

She placed her bike against a concrete wall, and reached a hand out to the cool stone of the cathedral steps and that recognition feeling of déjà vu came over her. She closed her eyes.

"You alright there?" asked the man, looking curiously at her from beneath his hood.

"Oh, yes. I'm admiring the architecture."

He looked doubtfully at the dark evening, and kept walking.

Sitting down with her back to the steps, she looked up, pulling her coat collar up around her face. A whooshing sound reached her ears and a jolt of knowing passed through her. She closed her eyes and drifted with it as the sky darkened and closed above her.

She was back on that hillside. It looked to be late afternoon and the colours were washed out in the grey day. The grass was dewy beneath her feet and fog hung in wisps. The woman picked her way down the path, holding a bundle, and Hazel prepared to follow.

A horse and cart bumped past, spraying mud at her. She jumped off the road, wondering if it would hit her. Mud in the main street of Dunedin. And the thick scent of silage like she was on a farm. Was this what the city used to be like? Hazel thought it was perhaps a hundred years ago or more.

The whole thing had been flattened so that Princes Street could run straight from the Octagon to South Dunedin. When she came around the corner, she gasped.

Instead of the square outside John Wickliffe House and

the low concrete planters in front of the grey and glass building, she was coming up to a dirt road roundabout. An imposing whitestone building stood in front of her with a clock tower. People strolled past, carrying bags or fabric. This was the bustling centre of town, with High Street and Princes Street branching off.

Even for a psychic witch who regularly listened to other people's thoughts, this was exciting. She itched to explore.

The woman was a fast walker. Hazel supposed she would be too, if that was her main method of transport. She hurried to catch up.

"Hello. Who are you?" she asked. But her voice faded into the background, inconsequential as a fly.

A gentleman got off a horse right next to her and she felt a flush rise up her face as she thought of what to say. Would 'good day' be appropriate? What about 'how do you do'? What year was she in? For that matter, could he even see her?

"She's stubborn, that old girl," he said, a broad grin on his face. Was he talking to her?

"Lavender?" the woman said from behind her.

Hazel struggled to listen but the fog swirled close around her, clinging to her clothes, her face, and the man and the building were no longer visible. The fog deepened to darkness, threatening to pull her in.

A moment of panic seized her, where she was swimming in the void. She thought down was up, and up was behind. Where was she? When was she? She struggled to bring the surroundings back, but could no longer remember. It was exactly like when you had a name on the tip of your tongue, but couldn't quite grab it.

She breathed deep, thinking of what she would do if she was caught in a 'rip' at the beach, and relaxed, letting herself float. Going with it.

She found herself back in the Octagon, back to the cold steps, legs prickling with pins and needles from sitting still.

After she stood up and brushed herself off, stamping her feet to get the blood flowing, Hazel jumped on her bike and pushed off slowly. It was a start. But it was obvious she was missing something.

<hr>

At home, she climbed up to the attic, as suspicion entered her mind of who the gentleman might have been talking about. She knew the visions were ancestral memories of the Redferne family. It was worth a try.

"Grannie," she said, out of breath. "Lavender Redferne. Who was she? Was there one?"

"Oh, hello, dear," Grannie Em said, looking up from her desk. She was checking on her pressed flowers today, smoothing the fragile pansy petals. "Yes. Lavender Ophelia Redferne. You don't know? She's my mother."

"Oh." She let out a breath. Her Grannie always talked of people who had passed away in the present tense. Hazel had not asked why. "What was she like?"

"Strongest woman I've ever known," she said. "Bit strict, of course. Thrifty as anything. And clever."

"And stubborn, would you say?"

"Oh, yes. Once she made me walk to school with only one shoe on. For two whole weeks, mind you, all because I lost it and then told porkies about it."

Hazel grimaced. "Poor little grannie Em," she said, with feeling. Lavender was her great-great-grandmother, she thought with a thrill. That didn't answer the other question, though. Who had she been following?

She chewed on her fingernail. "Did your mum have a sister?"

Em shook her head. "A brother," she said. She narrowed her eyes. "Are you having a séance? Without me?"

"No, nothing like that. I've been having visions. And I think I'm going to meet your mum."

On Thursday morning, Hazel tapped her fingers on the desk, and her eyes flicked to the door. She wondered if anyone else had noticed that Kirsten wasn't there.

Hazel had been chosen, along with June, Perry and Sia to present their ideas. Sia stood in front of the whiteboard, drawing a mind map in large red strokes. Perry was drumming his fingers on the table, impatient to get the meeting over. The bonus was so close he felt he could grasp it. Hazel's mind kept drifting to the visions, and when she could get back there.

A ding on her phone made her look down. An email had come through from Kirsten to the whole team. 'I won't make it to today's meeting. Something else has come up. Remember the tagline has to be intriguing and clickable. I'm sure I can trust you all to come up with something perfect.'

Hazel shook her head and placed her phone facedown on the table. The meeting time had already been moved once and this was supposed to be Kirsten's first appearance as their manager.

"Oh, apologies from our new boss," she said aloud to the others. She knew she sounded bitter, but it came down to the fact that you had to be able to trust people at their word. Otherwise, a witch might as well be flying in the dark, all alone.

"Really?" Sia put one hand on her hip. *I put off a lunch date with my husband for this. And it's our wedding anniversary.*

"Uh huh."

"Well, let's get on with it then. Hazel, will you take this pen and write a few ideas for each theme," Sia said, handing her a black pen.

'Call of nature,' she wrote, thinking of the rugged coast, windswept hills and hidden waterfalls. Her childhood visits to the peninsula with its gliding albatross and shy penguins. 'Nature at your doorstep.'

"The students would have a field day with call of nature, love," June said.

Speaking of the call of nature, Hazel thought. She passed the pen to Perry, who fumbled and dropped it on the floor.

This is my big chance to impress them all, Perry thought, as he bent down to pick it up. *Imagine my son's face when I say he can go to his basketball tournament. If I can just get this bonus.*

Slipping out the door, she crossed the office and went to the toilets, stopping briefly on the way back, relishing the quiet of the open space, after the clamour of voices and thoughts in the meeting room.

Hardly anyone was out here, and Kirsten's office was empty. The door was ajar. Did she dare to go in?

Hazel rocked on the balls of her feet, undecided. No, she didn't.

Or did she? Would this be her only chance to dig around? She grabbed a couple of dirty coffee cups, and placed them on the desk. If someone came past, she could pretend she was just gathering up dishes.

The office hardly looked used. Pens and staplers were in their place, and the pad on the desk didn't even have any doodles in the margins. She reached down into the bottom drawer and pulled it open, flicking the file dividers over until she found a notebook right at the back.

Hazel flipped through the notebook, looking over her shoulder every few minutes. The pages were pristine and tagged with labels. Hazel turned it around sideways to read them. 'Leads' was the first one. She put her fingernail in and opened up to that page. It was a huge list of names and email addresses. Some had notes written next to them. 'Not interested'. Some were crossed out, and some had ticks next to them.

The next label was 'Recipe'. A piece of old, yellowed paper was folded up inside, glued at the top. It was marked 'Margaret's Warming Drink' in spidery writing.

The next divider said 'Customers' and it was divided into three columns. The first column was again full of names. The second was titled Appointment and had dates underneath. The third was marked 'Sign up' and had ticks or crosses.

Hazel looked up, heart beating. She put her finger on the page under the very first name, 'Amanda Kennett'. Mandy. The second column had a date early last year, and the third column had a tick. She swallowed, thinking about what Mandy had told her about coming to New Zealand and getting the confidence mixture in return. 'Scott Hills' was there too.

So this was *the* notebook? Kirsten was taking advantage of people when they first moved cities, when they were vulnerable with thoughts of whether they had done the right thing. When they were feeling disconnected, mired in loneliness and low self esteem. And she was creating a dependence.

"Damn," Hazel said softly, staring into the space between the lines, until it blurred. It appeared that these people were being thrown a lifeline when they were really being pulled under. She needed to gather evidence. But the only way people got into the notebook was by moving to the city. Could Hazel ring up with a fake name?

She scanned the lines until she got to the bottom. 'Belinda Manitow' was the very last name and her appointment date was the very next day. She added the name and number into her phone and slipped out the door, picking up the coffee cups as she went.

Tomorrow, Hazel had to be at that appointment. But how was she going to pull this off?

———

She stopped to straighten her clothes, took a breath and slipped back into the meeting room. A heated debate was underway over whether coffee or tea was better. It was one of those meaningless little workplace discussions that could escalate quickly.

Hazel sensed the dark energy in the room, and spoke loudly, interrupting June's treatise on the benefits of the antioxidants in coffee.

"Okay," she said, trying to get the meeting finished quickly. "What do you think about 'Dunedin welcomes you'? Simple. Friendly." Four faces looked blankly at her.

She flicked through some of the notes she had written. "Or how about Dunedin Fresh?"

"Sounds cold," Sia said.

"It sounds like the name of a supermarket," Perry said.

"Alright, this is one I liked." He paused for effect. "'Come and breathe the clean air.'"

Hazel shook her head. They had been arguing for ages, and it didn't feel like they were getting anywhere. She could sense the desperation in the other three, who wanted the bonus badly, and she was about to give up. Leave them to fight over it.

"I don't think we want to imply that everywhere else is polluted," June said, taking a muffin from the plate in the middle. "What if we don't have the cleanest air in the country?"

People nodded. "What about... Enchanting?" Sia spread her hands with a flourish.

Hazel liked that, but June shook her head. "We can't over-sell it. Then people will just mock."

"Any publicity is good publicity, right?"

Hazel thought it was mostly because there were no snacks left, but everyone finally agreed. This was following two hours of brainstorming, and a further hour of refining drafts.

"'A Wild Welcome.' That'll do." Sia started packing up her laptop and folders into her bag. "Congratulations, Hazel! Now, let's get home."

Hazel sat back in her chair, while the others packed up their things. "Well done," June said to her as she left.

That evening, she typed up the proposal and the meaning behind it, and sent it through, while Joel was cooking dinner.

"Honestly, I think we would have gone for anything at that point," she said, over the hissing noise of the frying pan. "It wasn't even anything that special."

"I'm still so proud of you."

The smell of the steak searing made her stomach complain. "Thanks. I'm quite proud of me too. But I feel really bad for Sia, who works so hard. And what about Perry and his young son?"

"You can't help everyone, though," he said. "And you work hard too!"

She couldn't wait to see June's face when she gave her the money.

CHAPTER ELEVEN

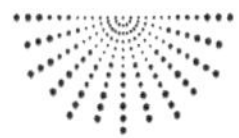

The little pride Hazel felt in her achievement changed quickly to anger the next morning.

Sia stopped in front of her desk, and it seemed like she wouldn't quite meet Hazel's eyes. She radiated sadness.

"Hazel, I came as soon as they told me. Look, I'm just going to come out with it. I've chatted to the bosses and they want to go with something a bit different."

"For the tagline?" She raised her eyebrows. It wasn't the first time she had come up with some great ideas that had been passed over. She hoped it was still based on one of the general themes they had decided on.

Sia pulled over a chair and sat down. She placed a piece of paper onto the desk between them, but kept her hand over it.

"They ran it past me first, and I agreed." *Didn't have much choice*, the thought floated to Hazel, as Sia lifted her hand.

The heading was printed in bright colours in a cursive script.

'Dunedin: What are you missing out on?'

Hazel read it through once, then again. She hated it. It wasn't friendly or informative. It didn't offer much of anything, simply asked a question for which there was no answer. She was sure she knew who had come up with that. It played on people's fears of missing out, and it left Hazel feeling vaguely uncomfortable.

"Um," she said, as a million thoughts rolled through her mind. A curly wisp of smoke rose up from the edge of the paper as her anger scorched it, and she quickly screwed it up. "Who approved this?"

Sia pointed upwards, indicating the powers that be.

"What about... the promised bonus?" she asked. It wasn't just about the money, it was the way the whole thing was handled. She wanted to complain about the hours that she had spent on this, that they had all spent on this. Time that they had taken away from loved ones. But it was no use. Sia already knew all of it. This would never happen with her in charge. It reeked of a certain woman with a blonde bob and a perfect, punchable nose.

Sia shrugged. "Don't ask me, love."

Hazel poured herself a coffee and thoughtfully dipped a Tim Tam biscuit into it, stirring the drink so that the chocolate melted on the outside.

After her first meeting of the day, she sat down to write a strongly worded email to Kirsten. She put her shoulders back, and narrowed her eyes at the screen, tapping out a few paragraphs. She paused, then copied Christo in. Was it too aggressive to send it to the big boss? Then she left the office, which is always the best move after sending a strongly worded email to management.

"Can you cover for me this afternoon?" she asked June on the way out. "Just say I'm at a meeting."

"Sure, sweetie," June nodded, her glasses bobbing on her

head. "Where are you off to? Spending some time with that sexy man of yours?"

"No, I wish I was. Just an appointment down at Brows."

———

Hazel checked out her reflection in the mirror. She had never used a Glamour before. Her brown curly hair and fringe looked as if it had never been styled. Her skin had a few age spots, and her nose was larger. She pulled the skin above her eye upwards to smooth the crow's feet at the edges.

A quick call to Belinda's number was all that was required. A shaky voice had answered.

"Hello?"

"It's Brows beauty salon. I'm sorry but we have to cancel your appointment today," Hazel said.

There was a pause. "Oh, okay then."

"We're short-staffed," she said.

"Oh, can I re-book in for next week?"

Hazel panicked. "Um, I don't have the book with me right now. We'll call you." And she hung up. This did not feel right, walking around wearing this woman's face while talking to her on the phone. It was beyond weird.

She sighed and tucked the phone into her handbag, thinking of Joel's face when he walked in last night. Fritha, her cousin, had been elbows deep in a concoction which smelled vaguely of sulfur. Hazel was chopping herbs. The kitchen was swathed in smoke.

"Hello babe," Hazel had said, smiling brightly to detract from everything that was happening.

He'd leaned against the doorway, eyes narrowed. "Red. What's going on?"

"Look, it's not what you think... Okay, it's exactly what you think." she finished. "We're preparing a little something. I thought you were heading to the gym?"

He mumbled something so low that she couldn't hear.

"What was that?"

"I dropped a weight on my foot," he said, moving his ankle around tenderly. "And didn't we have an agreement about... magic? That you at least give me a warning beforehand."

Was there a pause there, or was she imagining it? "I know, but Fritha has a new flatmate who's just moved in. And you were going to be out anyway. This really needs to be done tonight, so it's ready in time."

He walked through the kitchen, waving his arm at the smoke. "Do you ladies want a cider?" he asked, reaching into the fridge.

Hazel sighed, exasperated. His energy was disrupting their spellcasting. "We probably shouldn't drink and manifest. You go and watch something on the tv if you like."

When he was gone, Fritha pulled out a new candle from the box. "Tell me again, why didn't we send someone else along for the appointment instead? Like mum?"

"They know her. She supplies baked goods to the salon."

"Why couldn't you have just made up a name?"

"I tried that," she said, in a low voice. "They just offered me a facial and massage. It seems like only certain people are on the list. Like a bloody VIP party."

"Right," Fritha said, tongue between her teeth as she concentrated, carving the name into the candle. "Why Belinda? Why couldn't the name have been something like Ann? Three letters?"

Hazel plucked three hairs from her head, and added them to the mix. "That's just unfortunate."

Fritha blew off the wax shavings and set the candle down

in its holder. She poured the potion through a funnel into a small bottle and handed it to Hazel. "I so wish I could be there to see it. You're going to be amazing!"

Hazel smiled weakly. She had enjoyed drama in high school, but never thought the stakes for her acting would be this high.

When she left the office, she ducked into a public toilet, wrinkling her nose against the smell. She changed her top to a baggy shirt, and pulled out the candle and the bottle. A few drops of the oil splashed into the top of the bottle and she lit the wick with her lighter.

"Looking good," she said to herself, and went out the door. It was definitely one of the hardest spells she had done. Her mum and aunt had always called Glamours, Love Potions and curses 'tricky magic'. They didn't like anything that messed with identities or free will. Hazel tended to agree. In general.

Except that this was going to be used for good, to expose corruption. To bring down Kirsten's own personal empire.

What difference would a face make? She was still wearing professional clothes, a close-fitted skirt with soft satin lining, and business jacket.

On the inside, she was shaking. Terrified that someone would turn around, slowly raise a finger and yell "imposter!" She crossed the road and walked around the corner.

Nobody looked twice at her. She dropped a pill bottle out of her bag while reaching in to get her phone out at the lights. It fell onto the street with a clatter, and none of the three people waiting next to her even batted an eyelid.

She walked past the sign for Brows, pushing her

shoulders back, a confident older woman. She pulled the door open and walked up to the desk.

"Anthony please," she said, and turned away, tapping her fingers lightly on the table. What if Briar turned up while she was here?

"Your name?"

"Belinda Manitow."

Since her last visit, a bookcase had been slotted in next to the desk with a sign in curlicued writing, saying 'Brows Books'. It had a few literary titles and a lot of magazines artfully stacked in a zigzag pattern next to book stops in pale pink.

Hazel ran her fingers over the books, choosing one at random. She flipped it open, and turned to the door. She breathed out, realizing that nobody would recognize her. Kirsten herself could turn up if she liked.

Another woman nodded at her as she sat down.

"Belinda?" said the receptionist. "Come through here."

Hazel looked at the woman, and left it a fraction too long before she stood up.

Shit. That was her. "Sorry... my hearing." She gestured towards her ear, feeling absurd.

The woman led her down the wide corridor and stopped at a dark door. She opened it and stood aside for her to go in.

A man sat at a desk and soft music played in the background. He stood up and said, "Thanks for coming in. Would you like a hot drink?"

She sat down, taking her time, making sure to remember every detail. But all she felt was that her worries were drifting away.

"I'm Anthony," he said, drawing out the 'a' in a smooth deep voice so that she felt like she was being slathered in lotion. "So, first let me know what you're having trouble with. How has your move been?"

"I've been here for a few... months," Hazel said. "It has been a bit tough being older and trying to meet new people."

She had obviously said the right thing, as he leaned forward, almost eager. "That sounds hard."

"It is," Hazel said, fiddling with her bag on her lap.

"So you're finding it a bit lonely? Let me take that for you," the man said, hanging it on a hook behind the door. "We want you to be comfortable. Okay, so what do you think the biggest obstacle is for you? What is stopping you from joining, say, a dance club?"

Stay focused, she told herself. Play the part. "Well, I guess, I'm a bit worried I don't have anything interesting to contribute."

"Anxiety." He nodded. "You look tired, if you don't mind me saying. Are you sleeping well?"

She shook her head.

"Where did you move from?"

Hazel bit her fingernail as her mind raced. "Um, North." That should cover most of the country.

He looked down at his paper and frowned. "It says here Tapa— "

"Tapanui," she said along with him. Alright, so Belinda was from the South. "Yes, but it was the North part of town."

"And your appearance, does it match with how you feel on the inside?"

"Well, no," Hazel admitted, biting her lip to keep from laughing from nervousness. "I feel much younger."

Anthony smiled and a dimple appeared in his cheek. *Man, he is good*, Hazel thought. "So the great news, Belinda, is that we can help you. The question is, are you ready to turn your life around?"

"What I would recommend is our New You Treatment. You pay a low weekly fee for a minimum of three months. We provide you with microdermabrasion, any hair removal you need and our extra special treatment. It's a supplement to help with the mental side of things. This is cutting edge and exclusive to our clients."

"We can guarantee that you'll be feeling better within a month. We could even get started today if you like. I'll check with Beth out the front to see if we can get you slotted in as soon as possible. How does that sound?"

Bingo. So that was how the beauty salon fitted into the whole scheme? It was a complete package. A makeover and the Confidence spell. It was clever, Hazel thought, clever and horrible and wholly on brand for Kirsten.

She rearranged her face so that it looked impressed, instead of horrified. "That sounds really good, but... I'll have to book it in for another time." Hazel had to find out more about the scheme, but undergoing microdermabrasion, when she didn't need to, really crossed the line. Also she was sure it would mess with the Glamour.

"Okay, well we can get your payment started and forms done today." He produced a stack of white papers, neatly clipped together, the front page titled Non Disclosure Agreement. "There's an automatic payment form at the bottom. It's been lovely to meet with you, Belinda."

This was heavy-handed sales. Hazel felt like she was about to sign up for a gym membership that she didn't want and would never use. She felt sick, and more than halfway to being fooled.

"If you're not completely convinced, I can get my colleague Kirsten to talk to you." Anthony was leaning forward, and his smile was even wider.

And use her powers of suggestion to force people to sign up? No way. Hazel pulled the door open and stormed out.

CHAPTER TWELVE

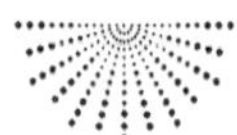

Hazel popped into the office a few minutes after five to pick up some work. There were still a few people around, chatting or working quietly. She hoped it wasn't anyone she knew.

She walked quickly to her desk then stopped for a minute to take some calming breaths. She had waited in the library for the Glamour to wear off, a thick book held up to her face. Just one mole on her chin remained the last time she checked in the mirror. A cold sweat trickled down her back.

"Oh, Hazel. I'm so glad I caught up with you." Kirsten appeared behind her. Her voice was low and calm. "You're a really slippery one."

"Getting a few things to catch up on over the weekend," Hazel said. "Ah, I have to—" She pointed down the hallway, desperate to get away. Why did Kirsten want to chat right now?

"About that email… I can see that you're not completely satisfied. We decided to go with a change of approach and everyone is really happy with it." Kirsten's eyes roamed over her face. "I'm sure you understand?"

Hazel pressed her lips together, thinking of June. "Well—"

"Don't look at me like that. We're both professionals," Kirsten said. "I know you've been poking into my business."

Hazel's heart started banging in her chest, and she swallowed the lump in her throat. How did she know?

"What do you... mean?" Hazel reached out with her mind to see what Kirsten wanted. She probed past her surface thoughts of work, past ideas of what she'd like for tea until... until she found an emptiness, dark and gaping. What could cause an emptiness like that?

"You're not the only one who can find things out. New boss." Kirsten pointed at herself with a self-deprecating smile. "People want to get onside with me."

Hazel didn't say anything, and suddenly the hum and whirr of the air conditioning was unbelievably loud.

"I'm not paranoid, but I am very careful around people who I know want to undermine me. Of course I went into my office to check if you'd been snooping. It wasn't hard to figure out. See, I'm very picky about how I like things," she said, lining up the papers on the edge of the desk as if to prove her point. "It's part of why I've been so successful. I don't do a half-assed job. Ever. And I notice when one of my drawers is open slightly. Because I would never leave it like that."

Hazel leaned back against the desk. She could relax a little. It didn't seem like Kirsten knew about the beauty salon, only that she had been into her office. Not great, but she could get out of it, she was sure.

"Admit it." That low, rolling voice seemed to echo around the space, and Hazel looked around to see if anyone else was listening. Nobody seemed to notice.

"Fine." She flashed her eyes defiantly. "I did go in there."

Sia popped her head around the corner with impeccable

timing. "Oh, there you are. Just reminding you that we've got that meeting in five minutes."

"Thank you," Kirsten said, sweet as pie. "You don't need to remind me, though. I have everything planned. Nothing ever sneaks up on me." She watched Sia leave, and turned back to Hazel.

"Your friend June told me that you were at a beauty salon appointment. I know where you were, but I haven't quite figured out how you did it. Yet."

Hazel gulped.

"Don't get involved in my business, Hazel Redferne. You've got one last chance to keep quiet. I have a feeling you're good at keeping secrets."

Her eyes settled on the mole, and Hazel had to force herself not to cover it with her hands.

"Oh, one last thing. Whatever gossip you've heard about a restructure? All true. I started the rumours." Kirsten held up two long fingers and brought them together in a snipping motion. "And if you can't keep your mouth closed, I can always recommend that Christo makes cuts to the staffing." She dropped this casually over her shoulder as she walked away. "He'll listen to me."

Hazel gritted her teeth. She did not like that woman.

The next morning, Joel looked carefully into her face, his brow creased with concern.

"You look shattered," he said. "Do you want to spend the day together?"

Hazel nodded. All of the responsibility and the worry laid heavy on her, and it would be nice to lay it all aside, if only for a few hours.

"But first, we're having breakfast." He made scrambled eggs and avocado on toast and set it in front of her. Hazel smiled gratefully.

"I'll make it next time," she said, adding, "If you don't mind it not being perfect."

"I can teach you to make this. It's easy as. And if you don't get it right the first time, we've got years for you to get it right."

He said it so calmly, and carried on eating. Inside, Hazel was singing.

"Do you want tea?" she asked, flicking the jug on.

"Mm hmm," he said, mouth full of toast. "I think this is the best breakfast I've ever made. Don't you?"

"Yeah, really nice," she said, looking at him strangely.

Hazel poured the water into the teapot and turned it three times, before leaving it to steep. It was his turn to watch her with a bemused expression.

"Would you like to go out?"

Just the two of them spending time together sounded perfect. "Yeah," she said. "Somewhere quiet. Somewhere beautiful."

They wrapped up in scarves and hats, and drove to the park in Arthur Street, and sat down on the slope, looking up at the conifers stretching into the sky.

Hazel slipped off her shoes and lay back on the grass. She turned her face, wanting to share something of herself. "Sometimes, when it's quiet, I can hear the earth breathe. Not as a whole planet but as a fragile... system." She didn't like that word because of its mechanical connotations, and struggled to explain. "Like a dandelion. Everything vibrates at its own frequency. Everything hums its own tune. Cities sometimes pull in all the good and suck you dry, but they sometimes pulse with life. People are storm clouds of ever-changing energy. Some disrupt the flow more than others, gathering bad energy around themselves like too many shopping bags."

He laughed, rolling onto his side. "What sort of energy do I have?" He lifted his arm up and flexed his bicep.

Hazel was quiet, feet flat on the grass, back pressed to the earth. The clouds were scudding across the sky in the Easterly wind. "When I first met you, it was as turbulent as the sea. And I knew you were lost."

Joel considered for a moment, then nodded in agreement. It was barely noticeable. "I was."

"But you would never have admitted that, then."

"No," he said. "I've done my best. You've helped me a lot."

A warm glow spread right above her breastbone, and she decided to ask one of the questions that niggled at her. "You once called me controlling. Do you... do you still think that?"

He took his time, putting the words together carefully, as if they were delicate. "The way I see it, you're like Google almost," he started.

"What? Why?"

"I'm not expressing myself very well. You... know everything. You're a mystery. You know what everyone wants, what everyone fears. You know what keeps them awake at night. It's natural that you'd want to help people."

"I've always wanted to help." She cast her mind back to the girls who had been her friends when she was twelve. These friends called her things like "know-all", "bossy" and "creepy" when she warned them which teachers to avoid because they were grumpy on a certain day or which areas of the school grounds to stay away from because they had a bad energy.

But Hazel had known when one of the girls was worried about asking the teacher for help because she had just started her period and a small bloom of red stained the back of her dress. She swapped uniforms with her in the toilets and bore the laughter of the other children.

She had known when her friend was uncomfortable sitting next to a boy who liked her, and had offered to swap places, which meant Ricky teased Hazel about her red hair for the next few months instead.

Other people would know these things, if they asked. They still had to care enough to help, though.

"You have your own way about you, Hazel. You take some getting used to, though," Joel said, pretending to wipe the sweat off his forehead.

"Stop it. You take some getting used to as well," she laughed.

"We've got time," he said simply, leaning over her so that his mouth was close to hers. Waiting. She lifted her head and kissed him quickly, then turned away.

"What is it?"

"I said you were like the sea before. But I think you might be the anchor." She threaded the grass between her fingers. "You remember when I zoned out in the Octagon?"

"Wasn't it just because you hadn't eaten?"

"No. No, that's not it at all." Hazel took a deep breath. "I can step into the memories of our family of witches." She looked around, guilty, but she wasn't struck down instantly by a goddess or any other deity for breaking the vow of secrecy. "I think I went into a memory of one of the Redferne women, one of my ancestors."

He opened his mouth, but she cut across him. Suddenly it was urgent. It was the most important thing she had to do. "I need to do it again, but I need you to hold me in place. Please."

He didn't ask any more questions, but he was very quiet

for the rest of the day. He started building the tiny house that
night, working until late on the back deck, with the light of a
camping lamp.

CHAPTER THIRTEEN

They held hands tight as they walked through the Octagon. It was as if they were each holding onto a life raft.

"It'll all be fine," she said.

"Yeah," he replied. "How are you always so optimistic?"

Hazel thought about it for a moment. "Because, although there is a lot of pain in the world, people are still trying to be good. People are mostly driven by love, and that is enough." And she had to be optimistic. Or she'd give up.

She told him to be ready to wait there for an hour with her. She had no idea how time passed when she was in the vision, but assumed that would be about right.

"Of course," he said. "I'll be here."

She looked down at their linked hands, and up at the cathedral. A feeling of peace settled over her. She could smell the clean, fresh scent of grass and the smell of coming rain and the light scent of smoke. This time, Hazel was lower down the hill and she looked down to see clover growing in the grass.

She heard a noise and the cart came rolling along the road, and flinched away as it rolled past.

Then when she looked up, the woman was hurrying down the path straight towards her. Hazel panicked for a moment, wondering if she should hide, but the reassuring grip of Joel's hand squeezed hers. This was it.

She turned away, until she heard the gravel moving on the path behind her. Would the woman notice her? Stop to talk? But the woman passed her by as she usually did, and Hazel crept slowly along behind.

It was mind-blowing, Hazel reflected. She was moving through a world without feeling the texture beneath her feet. But she smelled smells and heard sounds that were no longer there, whose last echoes had died away long since. She walked around the hill a way behind the woman, feeling Joel guide her gently off to the side. It had started to shower with a fine rain and the woman had put her cloak up.

Around the corner, Hazel was amazed again at the commercial centre of the town, a wide mud road lined with shops, and the large white stone building with its elegant arches rising up behind the Cargill Monument. She heard the sound of hammering, of stone striking stone, as people worked on buildings.

She hoped Joel was alright, and imagined him sitting with someone who would look, at best, like she had her head in the clouds, and at worst, like she couldn't handle her tequila.

Hazel stopped as the woman waited by the Cargill Monument, eyes narrowed at the carriages passing, hands on her hips. Hazel noticed a child walking along and watched him. He was dressed in short trousers and a little jacket, and stopped every now and then to dig the toe of his boot into the mud.

A man rode up on a beautiful dark brown horse,

dismounted and took off his hat. He led the horse off up a side street and Hazel walked along behind, excited. She was pretty sure by now that no-one could see her.

The noises of the horse's hooves and the hammering were somehow muted, which created a sense of peace. The sounds reminded her of fiddling with the tuning on the old radio speaker when she was young.

The man tied up the horse, pulled out a key and opened the door of a small house just up the rise. He stood out of the way and bowed to let the woman through, then ducked to get under the doorway. He held the door open for a minute, checking to see if anyone was following. His gaze swept over Hazel without faltering, and she crept forward before the door shut, slipping through into a small kitchen.

Hazel pressed herself against the wall, feeling scandalous in her modern clothes, although no one even glanced at her.

"I hope you've been keeping well," he said.

"I have, thank you. And you?" The woman was slight, and had a beautiful face. She put out a hand and collapsed into giggles when he grabbed it.

He grinned and kissed it. "Have you brought it with you?"

The woman reached into her skirts, producing a small bottle tied with twine and stopped with a piece of cloth. The man took it, and brought it up to his face to peer inside.

"Oh, you're the best," he said. "A lady of surpassing goodness."

"I am," she said, and preened. "This is one of the last few bottles, though. We have to make some progress and smartly."

The man nodded, and tucked the bottle into his jacket. He reached over, grabbed a ladle and scooped it into a pot on the stove. A congealed mess slopped into the bowl. Hazel thought it smelt like it could have been chicken soup at one point.

She followed the couple up the stairs and a cool breeze reached her, like a window was open. It was at the end of the hall, and the sash was lifted a little. It ruffled her sleeves.

It was then that she realized that she had lost Joel's hand. *Oh Goddess.* Where was he? How would she get back? Hazel stopped still on the landing, one hand on her chest, thinking of that terrifying blackness.

"Lavender," the man called. He unlocked a door off to the side.

Hazel couldn't stand the curiosity. In for a penny, in for a pound. She crept forward to see. Inside was another woman, sitting on the bed. She was curvy and had dark reddish brown hair hanging loose around her face and the rough hands and muscled forearms of a hard-working woman. She got to her feet as soon as they opened the door.

"Yes," she said, not shrinking away from him. Hazel scanned everything, trying to commit it all to memory. It was a strange atmosphere. All three seemed wary of each other, but none seemed weaker than the rest.

"Have something to eat," he said, thrusting the bowl of cold soup at her. Was he keeping her locked away up here?

She took the bowl and ate it slowly, eyes flicking between the both of them. "What are you doing up here, Daisy?"

"I just want to talk to you," Daisy said.

"You know I don't feel the same," Lavender retorted, eyes flashing.

"God, I'm glad you gave me the confidence to put you in your place," said the man. He was nervously brushing at his dark hair to smooth it down. "No husband wants to be made a fool by his wife."

Hazel watched, aghast. That was Lavender's husband? Keeping her up here, feeding her cold soup?

"You're a coward through and through, John," Lavender said. "No potion is going to change that—"

The man flinched and his nostrils flared. Daisy frowned. "Give me the secret of the spring," she commanded, stepping forward. It was a voice that was used to obedience. A voice that sent shivers up Hazel's spine.

Lavender put a hand to her mouth. "Up by the... " she began, slowly, her face reddening, as if she didn't want to say it.

"Come on. I need to make some more."

"It's ours," Lavender croaked, bending over with the effort to resist the voice. Hazel wanted to run to her.

"The secret of the spring," came the awful voice.

Lavender straightened, sweat running down her face and making dark blotches around the neck of her dress. The veins stood out on her face.

She intoned a spell, in a strong voice, and Hazel watched in amazement as Daisy went pale.

The man pulled Daisy roughly from the room by the hand and slammed the door.

Lavender brushed her hair out of her face and looked right at Hazel. "This is what I wanted to show you, love. Do you understand?"

She nodded. "I think I do."

Then Hazel was lost in the dark, falling, floating. She couldn't breathe. She fought to stay upright, as the void threatened to drown her. Pulse racing.

Follow what scares you, she remembered. She stopped fighting and let it pull her downwards.

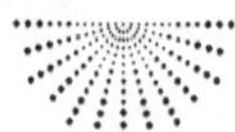

CHAPTER FOURTEEN

*H*azel's vision cleared. The clouds receded and the noise and bustle of midday in the present time came back to her all at once. The cold of the steps chilled her to the bone. But she was alive.

Joel was nowhere to be seen. She pulled out her phone. Only twenty minutes had passed since she went into the vision. She rang him, wanting to share all the feelings of triumph, pride in her ancestor and now desolation. There was no answer. Where was he?

The bus ride up the hill felt interminable and a headache was already starting just above her right eyebrow.

The house was quiet. Hazel pushed open the door and stepped inside. She couldn't sense Bonnie in the house through her familiar connection but she was in the neighbourhood somewhere.

"Joel?"

The floorboard just inside the door felt springy under her foot. She bent down to look. Where the floor and the wall met, toadstools were growing into the house, their springy stalks cracking the gap in the floorboards. They definitely weren't there yesterday. She grimaced. Something definitely wasn't right in the energy around here.

Bonnie trotted in the front door. Her tongue was hanging out of her open mouth.

"What are you— "

At the bottom of Joel's garden. Kirsten. Now.

Hazel ran over to the gate, but her hands were shaking so much, she couldn't open it. Breathe, she told herself. She forced herself to take two deep breaths, then tried again. The gate opened easily this time and she flew past the bushes and over the flattened ground where the cabin used to be, past the tumbledown garage covered in weeds, down the hill. She thought she heard a noise further down, and slowed her pace as she crept through the gap in the pittosporums.

The fruit trees were bare, waving their grey arms at the slate sky. What on earth was Kirsten doing here now?

She slipped a little in the mud as she reached the bottom of the garden. The old dinghy was empty. No-one was there, and all looked well.

Where was Kirsten headed?

Of course. The well. It was covered with a wooden top for safety. She lifted the peeling brown top off and eyed the gloomy depths. It was difficult to tell how deep it was. She picked up a rock and threw it in, then climbed over the side and dangled one leg over. There was a ladder in the side and she lowered herself into the narrow space. Her feet touched the slimy bottom, just as she got to the point where her arms were stretched. And something cold oozed into her shoes. Yuk, it was stagnant water. She lifted a shoe up and splashed it down again.

It was pitch black down here, with the round of daylight above her head. She turned and cast around with her hands, and found some smooth wood. It was a sort of door and she

slipped her fingers around the side and tugged at the edges to
pull it out. She had to bend over to get through. Before she
did, she stopped to listen for any sounds, but there was
nothing except the faint drip of water.

She crept forward, bent over, now and then putting her
hand on the ground for balance but regretting it, as it was
smelly and wet. The tunnel seemed to be made from packed
earth and it wasn't very long. The rest of the time she held
her hands in front. After about ten steps, her hands touched
wood again. She pushed the next door and stepped through.
A faint light showed that she was in a cave. The ground was
uneven but at least she could stand straight here.

A wide ledge curved around to the left, with light stone
on the right. The light was coming from a grill far above.
Hazel wondered where it was, maybe further up the hill from
her house. She stepped forward, wiping her hands on her
pants, and as her eyes adjusted to the light, she saw a darker
spot on the ground and an old suitcase.

Walking forward, she looked over the edge. This was the
trickling sound she had heard, as the water trickled over the
edge into a thin stream, which must be the magical stream
that ran between their properties.

A pit of sand and gravel had a broken egg shell sitting in
it. This must be where the lizards lived. Hazel's heart sped up
as she searched the cave.

Kirsten had told them that the lizards had to be kept in
their habitat or they would all die.

Hang on, why was there a suitcase down here? Hazel
knelt down next to it, looking at the old leather, which was
flaking off in places and covered in a light white dusty film. It
was more of a trunk really. She opened it up and lifted out an
off-white linen quilt. Underneath was some papers and a few
old flasks, and a cast iron plate.

She couldn't resist flicking through the bundle of old letters. She opened one carefully, and sat back on her haunches.

My dear Lavender.

At the mention of Lavender, Hazel's skin tingled.

She scanned the letter; discussions of people she didn't know, the intricacies of an everyday life long forgotten. Near the bottom, the mention of secrets made her look closely.

Although they no longer use the name, there are those who seek to use our secrets.

You will be safe for a short period in that place where we played. Never tell anyone of its location, even those you hold most dear. That is the most important. We take the secret to our graves.

I pray you take caution, my dearest. Do not trust anyone. As soon as I have found a solution, I will fetch you.

Your loving and most devoted brother

Gerald Redferne

She sat down on the cool stone, listening for any sounds. The only noise was the water. It was a calming spot and the cool, dry air was comfortable. It felt safe. This must be the secret place he talked about.

All of this was enough for someone to live down here for a couple of days at a time. But why were they staying down here?

Hazel tucked the papers into her waistband, and turned back. It was clear she was too late for the lizards.

***

By the time she pulled herself back up the well, toes scrabbling for purchase on the stone, dangling there for longer than she wanted to admit, it was late in the afternoon.

Bonnie clamped onto her sleeve and yanked. Hazel's muscles screamed as she pulled herself back up.

The grey sky had turned to white, and the trees were creaking in the wind.

Oh, you stink, Bonnie growled.

"Thanks. Now you know what it's like when I can smell wet dog," she said.

She hurried up the hill, Bonnie following at her heels.

When she got back to the house, she pushed the front door.

"Joel," she called. "Are you here?" She walked through to the kitchen, trying to dispel the feelings of disappointment and worry. Was he avoiding her? Was the magical side of her getting too strange for him?

She went into the bathroom and ran the hot water in the basin, looking at herself in the mirror. She had mud streaked down the sides of her face, mud on the backs of her hands and arms, dark grey in her red hair. Turning her face side to side, she decided she kind of liked the swamp hag look. She grabbed a facecloth and rubbed it over her face, holding it in place and letting the steam warm her. That was a bit better. But she was leaving the hair streaks.

"So, Bonnie, we have a cave on Joel's property that leads to the magical stream. But there were none of those lizards down there." If it was that easy to access, how come Kirsten hadn't taken the creatures before? Something must have changed.

She poured water into the jug and flicked it on to boil, watching the dog thump her tail on the ground as she listened to Hazel.

She took down her favourite teapot and added dried rosehips and a little mint to the infuser. She poured the hot water and a fragrant scent rose up around her. She turned the teapot three times, and left it to steep.

"And why has nobody ever told me about the cave before?" Surely someone knew about it. Joel? Her Grannie? No, when Bonnie had brought one of the creatures home in her mouth, she wasn't even aware of the lizards. Briar? She had lived here for years. She must know of it, if not exactly where it was. But a rumour, maybe. Hell, she would even settle for a whisper of it.

She looked up the name Daisy, and tapped her fingers on the keyboard. It was useless. She only had a stupid first name. She accidentally tapped on 'Enter' and the search results came up. Daisy is a nickname for Margaret. Well, that was very interesting. Margaret's Warming Potion maybe?

Hazel poured out the tea, and added a little honey. Thinking of how her mum used to make this for them, she savoured the hot, slightly tart drink. Suddenly everything felt a little better.

She rang through to her aunt. "You've reached Briar," she heard. "Call me on the cafe phone or leave a message." It didn't even ring, so she must have let her mobile run out of charge. Hazel made a note to hassle her aunt about being hard to get hold of.

CHAPTER FIFTEEN

Feeling a little bit better, Hazel decided to have a quick shower to get rid of the rest of the smell. Then she would try calling Joel again.

As she lathered her hair with sweet smelling jasmine shampoo, she reflected that it was extremely odd that Joel had chosen that moment to go somewhere else. She trusted him to be there for her, to anchor her in the present. She needed him. And he had left, without even sending her a message. What could possibly be so important? The more she thought about it, the more suspicious it seemed.

Shivering, she threw on her favourite grey hoodie, a present from her cousin, which read "When I go for a walk at night, I get moonburn." across the front. It had the word 'Redheads' on the back. She pulled on a pair of comfy black yoga pants.

Hazel stopped to throw her arms around Bonnie's neck.

"That feels much better," she murmured, nuzzling her face into the soft fur around the dog's neck.

Now you smell like a flower garden. You need to go roll in something on the grass, you know, so your prey can't smell you coming.

"Uh, no," she said, sitting down on the couch. Bonnie jumped up beside her, resting her head on Hazel's leg, and she patted her automatically.

"Right," she said, and took out her phone. She dialled Joel, but his phone just rang, before the answering machine started.

She clicked her tongue. Why couldn't she get hold of anyone today?

Bonnie was staring at her, head on her paws.

Hazel leaned back against the arm of the couch and swung her feet up. She sank back into the cushions and closed her eyes to get her swirling thoughts into some sort of order. It had to be all connected. Daisy. Also known as Margaret. And her great-great grandmother Lavender.

The visions happened when her subconscious was triggered by something. The cathedral. The baby photo! Perhaps it was something to do with Kirsten.

She searched for Margaret, adding Kirsten's surname, Treleaven, and put in Dunedin and the year from the picture she found, 1885, for good measure.

Hazel squinted at the screen. The results were images of newspaper pages, with tiny letters cramped in boxes. She zoomed in and scanned the words quickly.

Under an advertisement for Peter Atkinson's Best Cod Liver Oil and next to Cockles Pills - Free from Mercury, she spotted what she was looking for, under the column Miscellaneous Wants. 'Nervous disposition? Indigestion? Apply to M Treleaven for guaranteed help.' Well, that certainly sounded witchy.

She found a Death Notice next. It simply read: Margaret

Deed nee Treleaven. At Dunedin, on the 14 August. The date at the top of the newspaper was 1899.

The next link was a family tree. She squinted closer at her phone. Margaret Deed was married to Harold Deed. She traced the line down, through different surnames. Then at the very bottom on the left, she found Kirsten Treleaven.

Bingo, Hazel thought. She scratched absently at her shoulder.

Kirsten's parents' surname was O'Connor. So was her sibling. She was married to a Kennett. For some reason, though, she had taken the family surname Treleaven. Interesting!

Hazel looked closer. She scrolled across. Kirsten's sibling was called Timothy O'Connor. The boy had died in 1986. And his birth date was 1981. Tears pricked at the corner of Hazel's eyes as she realized he had died at 5 years old. She remembered again the emptiness Kirsten was holding. Grief could cause some of that. She had seen something similar in Joel.

Absorbed in her research, she thought nothing of the tiny pricks in the skin of her back. Suddenly it was insects, crawling all around her, sticking their teeth in, until a spiky, itchy feeling covered her body. She was drowning in creeping, crawling insects.

She stood up before she knew what happened, letting out a little scream, brushing her body off, shaking her arms and stamping her feet. She looked at the couch cushion and saw a few tiny insects, scattering to hide in cracks and under cushions. What were they, bedbugs? Lice?

"Bonnie, get off there!"

The dog jumped off, then stood next to the couch, neck stretched, nose sniffing.

I was only kidding before about rolling in something.

Her grannie Em poked her head through the ceiling. "What's all the commotion? I was trying to finish off my thesis."

Hazel bit back all of the questions that this statement raised, and gestured to the couch. "These... tiny little bugs. They were biting me, I'm sure of it."

"Ooh, interesting. See if you can catch one, and I'll have a look."

Hazel grimaced. "If I must." She lifted a hand and a glass flew from the kitchen and into her grasp. "Perfect catch. I've been working on that."

She threw the couch cushion off, and looked for the tiny bugs, but couldn't see any. Leaning on the couch, she craned her neck to see down the side of the seat. And felt a prickle in her hand. Ugh, one of the small brown things had bitten her. She plucked it off with her fingernail and quickly placed the glass over top. She grabbed a book off the coffee table and held it tightly over, then replaced it with plastic wrap in the kitchen. She held it up, and the insect was racing around the base, small and brown, with sort of a white shimmer around it.

Up in the attic, Grannie Em rubbed her silvery hands together. "I love these mysteries. They give an old lady something to be excited about."

Hazel placed the glass on the desk. "So, you're writing a thesis?"

Em ignored her. "I've got my microscope out ready, dear" she said, clearing some space on the desk next to what looked like an antique microscope. This involved pushing books and papers into a messy, overflowing pile. Em transferred the bug into a watch glass and added some solution from a dropper.

"Alright... Very interesting... Well, I can see it's a parasite, already. See its little proboscis?" She adjusted the focus again, and Hazel leaned across to have a look. "But... what sort, I do not know. Looks to be similar to a mite. Did Bonnie get bitten too?"

Hazel shook her head and a shiver of disgust ran up her body. "I don't think so."

"Have you been anywhere different, next to stagnant water or anything?"

Emily rolled up the sleeves of her silvery nightgown, squinting her eyes and nodding her head, while she listened as Hazel explained. "Bonnie saw that Kirsten woman down by the well. Of course I was worried about the lizards. I went to have a look and ended up climbing down the well."

"Whatever for, dear?"

"Grannie, I was right. There's a secret tunnel to a cave down there. And it was a way to access the magical spring. You never knew about it?"

She shook her head. "No, I never heard anything about it. And I've *lived* here for over 100 years, for lack of a better word."

"That's really weird. Oh! And look at this." She passed the letters over to Em, who took a look at the front page. Her translucent throat seemed to swallow as she leafed through, looking at the names.

Hazel looked through the microscope again to give her a minute.

"What a treasure trove! I've found one you might like to look at, dear," she said.

Hazel took the paper and sat on the bed. It was another one from Gerald to Lavender. Short and to the point.

I've done it. I have figured out the Secret Keeper spell. We can keep our family legacy safe. This is especially wonderful for you, dearest. Find a plain bauble and we shall enchant it. Hazel touched the locket at her neck. They had succeeded.

There is only one problem, this being that secrets are never destroyed, only passed down through generations in the coven. If the secret is forced, the role will be passed down. As there is need, so the next Secret Keeper will be initiated. It is perfect.

Gerald Redferne

Hazel and Em stared at each other, eyes shining with tears. Each lost in their own thoughts. Had Briar given up the secret? Was that why it was now Hazel's turn?

"Your father? What was he like?" Hazel hoped dearly that the man she had seen was not Em's father. But how could he not be?

"I don't remember him very well," she admitted. "It was always my uncle who turned up when we needed him."

Suddenly, Em brought her hands together, businesslike again. "Well, it simply won't do for me to be sentimental. I'd never get anything done." She put her eye back to the microscope. "I think you've brought the parasites back with you in the mud. Look how it shimmers white, though! I don't think it's sucking blood. So that begs the question, what is it sucking? Leave it with me, dear. I will not sleep - ha! - until I've figured it out."

Hazel went back down the ladder, and couldn't shake the feeling that something was crawling up her back.

She looked down when her phone vibrated in her hand. It was an incoming call from Joel. *Finally*, she thought.

"Hey. What happened to you?"

Joel cut her off. "Hi, can you meet me in town?"

"Sure. I can bike down if you need me to," she said, doubtfully. "Whereabouts are you? Could you take a taxi?"

"Write down this address," he said, "and come as soon as you can, please."

Hazel rang off, and looked at her familiar. Bonnie cocked her head to the side as Hazel spoke.

"Joel's stuck in town."

Where has he been all afternoon?

"I'm... not sure." He hadn't had time to answer any questions. In fact, he hadn't sounded much like himself at all, speaking fast, talking over her. Suddenly Hazel didn't feel great about the situation.

What if it's a trap? Bonnie asked.

Hazel considered. "Well, I mean, if Kirsten wanted to trap me, she could do it at work."

I don't like this, Hazel. At least let me come along.

"It's too far for you to walk. If it's a trap... well, I'm not sure. But I can't leave him there." She thought for a second. "I could ring Fritha. Ask her to pop by and pick you up?"

Good idea.

If Kirsten was waiting for her... Well, Kirsten was a person, just like anyone else. She was her boss. What could she do?

But it wouldn't do to be too naive either. Hazel hesitated in the hallway.

She put her phone to her ear. "Hey Fritha," she said, when her cousin picked up. "Can you help?" She explained that Joel had called her, after leaving in the middle of the vision.

"Wha— ? He wouldn't leave you, would he?"

Hazel tucked the jar of parasites into her bag. "I don't think so, either. And I'm not just going in there blind. I do have some sort of a plan," she said. Well, it was the beginning of a plan. It just hadn't quite come together.

"You can't go in there alone, Hazel. We've got to get a team of people together, like a fellowship," said Fritha.

"Look how well that turned out. Look, she's my boss. She needs me. And I don't know that many people," Hazel added, wandering into her room and bending down to get her grandmother's grimoire out from under the bed. "Let alone powerful, magical people. That are available on short notice. And don't have to go to work."

"Well, there's me," Fritha said.

"That's one."

"Two! We must know some more."

Hazel nodded. She wondered how much use a kitchen witch and an empath witch would be in a combat situation, and racked her brains for other ideas.

"Right," she said, "and there's a woman who lives across the road who can do a pretty mean hex."

"Is that the one who enchanted your bike helmet?"

"Yeah, she is mostly retired, but I'll ask her. Better still, I'll give you her number." Diana was an imposing woman with bold features and a commanding voice. She called herself a freelancer, and could be quite forbidding if you were on the wrong side of her. But on the same team...

"Three is a powerful number," Fritha said. "I'll go get help and meet you there."

"I'll probably get there and he'll be waiting in a hotel room in his birthday suit," Hazel joked. She couldn't seem to help making jokes when fear gripped her.

"Hope not! We will be there as soon as we can," Fritha said. "You can do this. You're the strongest witch I know."

She rang off, and Hazel put her phone down to get a good grip on the heavy grimoire. Her parents had left the book here when they came to visit, and Hazel was supposed to be teaching herself all of the spells inside. But who had time for that on top of everything else?

When Hazel picked the grimoire up, a handful of bugs scattered in all directions on the wooden floor and she stepped back. It almost seemed like the bugs were attracted to magical things. Struggling to hold it in one hand, Hazel found the right page and memorised a quick attack spell.

She found one of the bugs, dead, trapped between the pages, and held it between her fingers. Then went into the kitchen and popped it into a plastic bag, meaning to give it to her grannie later.

She headed out the door, thinking this day couldn't get any stranger. She was wrong.

 Warmed by the confidence Fritha had in her, Hazel biked to the address in town. She couldn't see Joel anywhere outside. *Big surprise,* she thought, but cold fingers snaked down her spine as she realized that she had no idea what she was walking into. She chained her bike up to the fence. The building was shut up and no signs of life showed in the windows. She scanned the building, looking for any other way in. Iron fencing covered the gaps to either side, so there was no way to get in any other door. Talk about secure.

No, she said to herself. Give up any thoughts of sneaking in and being some sort of hero. This isn't a novel.

She climbed the steps, hesitating only for a moment, and tried the wide wooden door, pulling on the ring. It didn't budge, so she knocked.

The door opened slowly, and Joel stepped out from behind it. A wide corridor with 80's carpet halfway up the walls led straight ahead and a door to a stairwell stood off to the right.

"Hi," she said to Joel. "Is everything alright?"

"Hello," he said. He didn't reach for her. "Come this way, Hazel, but listen... " He paused. "It's not... what you think." He looked at her significantly, raising his eyebrows.

"Are we in da..." she started to ask, but he placed his hand over her mouth.

He looked seriously at her. "Please just give her a few minutes."

Her who? He led her down the hallway and she followed along, nervous as hell, but since she was with Joel, she knew she would be alright.

Kirsten was sitting at a desk in the far corner of the room. Hazel felt a sort of relief as all her worry, all her fear, was proven to be right. This was followed swiftly by the type of fear that clings to your spine with cold, clawed fingers.

"You do know who that is, right?" she whispered to Joel.

He just nodded, then flopped into a chair next to her, looking like he was hanging out with a friend.

"You and I are the same, Hazel," Kirsten said, smiling at her. "We both can't stand to be taken by surprise by these things."

"Kirsten," Hazel said, her voice flat, keeping her eyes fixed on Kirsten's grey dress while trying to check if Joel was alright. "Not the same."

Kirsten put her hands out. "Stay calm," she said. "Joel came to me of his own accord."

"No, he didn't," she spat. "You grabbed him away while I was... busy."

Kirsten turned to him. "Joel?"

He nodded, almost sheepishly. "She needed me to come. And I owe her."

That hurt like a blow to the chest. She struggled to know where to look or how to stand, as the floor seemed to tilt away.

"I asked him to come here today." So that was it. Kirsten had used her voice to force him to come - right when she was in the middle of a vision?

"And Briar?" Kirsten looked to the side, where her aunt appeared from a doorway. "You came to me, didn't you?"

"I did."

Hazel looked from Briar to Kirsten to Joel, and a whooshing noise started in her ears as confusion turned to panic. Were they all against her? How could they do this?

"Have a seat, sweetie," Briar said, and Hazel sank into the chair. "I was really curious about the Confidence potion since you told me about it, and the idea kept playing on my mind. What if it could help me in the competition? I know it's silly. Kirsten here thought I'd be a great partner who could refer people through the cafe. A win-win for us both."

"But that's stupid!" she blurted. "Kirsten attacked you!"

"What?" Briar shrugged.

"Ancient history," Kirsten said, with a shrug.

"My cousin recommended the Confidence potion," Joel said. "I thought it couldn't hurt to give it a shot. It was about a week ago."

"I know I've gone about this a roundabout way, alright, a sneaky way, asking your partner and aunt here first. But I want to give you all the opportunity to be part of the business."

"What business?"

"I'll tell you about my wee magic formula," she began. "Because I really hope you'll join us. It took me a long time to refine it from an old family recipe, so that it didn't have the nasty side effects. It's called Confidence, and it quite simply gives the person who drinks it more confidence in their own abilities. It can have good effects on their love life, work life, family relationships, and in their own wellbeing. It helps people recognize the skills and attributes they *already have*."

"I'm really proud of the work that I did. I come from a science background, so it was a mix of research and the scientific method, as well as some magical help. I trialled it on a large group, with mixed results. If used in certain individuals, it can inflate their confidence without the necessary skill level to back it up. But overwhelmingly, it has *helped* people, Hazel."

Kirsten was walking up and down, waving her arms.

"The hardest part of the whole thing has been sourcing a good supply of the lizard blood. I am really passionate about the environment, and never want to disrupt any species. But I needed to ensure they didn't die out, and in fact, thrived."

"Well, once I secured the purchase of Joel's property, it was a weight off my mind. But I knew I wanted to take it bigger."

She stood up and walked to the back of the room and pulled open a door. "Come with me and I'll show you." Briar and Joel didn't hesitate, so Hazel followed.

The door led to a concrete stairwell and at the bottom was a locked white door. They all paused on the landing while Kirsten put in the code. Hazel grabbed Joel's hand. Another unmarked door stood in front of them.

Kirsten unlocked it, and stood at the side, waiting for them to pass. It seemed like they were in a basement, since there were no windows. Three glass tanks as tall as Hazel stood along one side, half filled with small stones and sand. Bits of wood and small plants completed the picture. It looked just like the reptile house in a zoo.

Memories of her dream spiked a warning at the very top of her spine, the primitive part of her brain telling her to get the hell out of there.

"I had to figure out a way that I could make the creatures breed in a captive environment. So I've brought them here to a mimicked habitat."

Hazel was silent. It was surreal standing here with these people. She still felt vaguely on the back foot, like she'd turned up to a party when everyone had been talking about her beforehand and stopped just as she entered the room.

Kirsten was putting on rubber gloves, and Hazel followed as she walked down towards the end of the tanks, where a smaller tank sat with an open top. A perspex tunnel lead from the closest tank.

"We encourage them down here so we can take their blood, gently, under controlled circumstances. Only a little at a time."

The only sound was the gentle bubble of water in pipes. How could an environmental expert keep the creatures in cages like this?

"Beforehand, I had to take as much as I could at one time. And once, I went a little too far. That isn't going to happen anymore."

Hazel thought of the dead lizard Bonnie had found, its silver blood trickling from its body. Her heart started pumping strongly in anger, but Kirsten went on.

"I've always wanted to do something great. Something that *means* something, haven't you? Now we are turning a profit of $100,000 a year, up 50% on last year. It is still small fry compared to some of the tech companies. But really, what price tag can you put on getting your life back?"

"You're asking me?" Hazel was shaking with anger. Joel squeezed her hand gently. "Well, my question to you is, should you do this just because you can? And because this formula has positive effects for some, does it mean that all the others aren't important? Who died and made you a goddess?"

Hazel pretended to think, facing away. She couldn't see Kirsten as anything but her boss. And she had to admit that she didn't want to lose her job. She had to stay calm.

She looked around at Joel and her aunt, checking to see if they were listening. "What about all of the people that you have convinced to come here to Dunedin? Those people you've locked into a contract for your formula by making sure they are unhappy? You're taking away control over their lives."

"Really?" Briar asked.

She saw Kirsten falter for the first time, and was happy to see her face pale. She pressed her advantage.

"Is that because of the partnership with Christo? Is it for mutual benefit? Those poor people moving cities, feeling lonely. He sells them properties through Passé Developments, while you sell the formula to them once they arrive?"

"Is that right?" Joel asked.

Briar put her hands on her hips.

"We don't want to get involved with something like that," Hazel said.

"I think we can put all of that to one side," Kirsten said, enunciating the last words clearly.

Briar nodded, and Hazel regarded her curiously. Was her aunt not understanding everything Kirsten had done to get here? The disregard for people? And magical creatures?

"These two are fans of the Confidence potion, Hazel. I'm sure you'd like to hear them tell you about what it can do."

Hazel's heart was beating in her throat. She swallowed heavily. Joel didn't seem to want to meet her eyes.

"You know as well as anyone how good social proof is for convincing people," Kirsten said.

Yes, Hazel thought. Social proof was when an advertiser showed that other people were happy with a purchase. It could be reviews or ratings. It could be infomercials where immaculately-groomed women in huge houses assure the audience that they love their vacuum cleaner more than life itself.

"It does work very well," Briar said. "That potion. I can think of so many things it could be used for."

Hazel turned to the closest tank to give herself a moment to think.

"The deal would be a 5% share for each of you, in return for becoming agents. So, let's get the documents signed and we can all be on the same side."

Did Kirsten really think Hazel would want to be her partner? She was not a very good boss. Hazel already knew that. Was Kirsten that deluded or was it all another way to control her?

"What's the catch?"

"No catch."

Joel and Briar seemed to be thinking on their own. But Hazel remembered that Kirsten had forced her to do things with her voice before. She was suddenly sure that she was the only one who could resist it.

She reached deep inside, murmuring the spell she had learnt. She managed to draw all her power in, compressed it to a hard ball, then released it as she turned towards Kirsten, all her energy focused on knocking her back.

Kirsten flinched out of the way, when she saw Hazel's movement. But it fizzed between them with a pathetic noise. Pfft.

Hazel turned her hands over and looked at them. Her

magic chose now to go on the fritz? She tried again, but nothing happened. Was this the punishment for breaking her vow of secrecy?

Kirsten let out a breath, and straightened. "I thought you had me there. Here's me trying to have a civilized conversation and you're attacking?"

Déjà vu grabbed Hazel as Kirsten moved beside Joel. She was going to stab him. Hazel's heart sped up, and she prepared to run forward, although she had no idea what she could do without her magic.

"I'm disappointed," Kirsten said. "I'll admit it. Aren't you, Joel? I thought you'd be convinced by having two loved ones here. I was sure you'd join us."

Hazel watched nervously. Any time now, Kirsten would lunge for Joel. But nothing happened.

"I warned you." Kirsten walked around Hazel, lifted two long fingers and made a snipping motion. And Hazel knew, even as her heart sank, what it meant. She no longer had a job. Well, there was no going back now.

Was the dream just a symbol? Dreams were as curly as her aunt Briar's cinnamon twists. It hadn't been warning her that Joel would be attacked. The knife in the back meant that he was the one that would betray Hazel. Why hadn't she listened?

CHAPTER SEVENTEEN

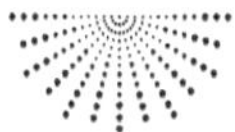

Hazel stood there, fists clenched in anger, staring at them for a moment. Then she remembered the plan. Delay. Distract. Keep her talking about anything.

"I've got something to discuss with you," she said, taking the plastic bag out of her bag and dumping the insect onto the desk. Briar and Joel came closer to look.

"What is this?" Kirsten demanded, craning her neck to see.

"It's a parasite. I think you've upset the balance," Hazel said, her voice quiet.

"Parasite?" She could see the interested gleam in Kirsten's eyes.

"And it started even before you took the lizards from their home. I think it began when you took Joel's land with the magical spring where the lizards live." She explained about the bugs running wild and the fungus growing into her house.

"I wonder," Hazel started, then stopped. She remembered the itching bites, and the white glow around the fat bug they had observed. Parasites needed a food source. Well, that made sense. "I think that these bugs might suck the magic out of things. That's why I couldn't do anything before."

"Interesting."

"That land is supposed to come under our protection, the protection of the Redferne coven. And something hasn't felt entirely *natural* for a while. Living things, like plants and insects, know when things aren't right. You're an environmentalist, you should understand. The population of this bug shouldn't be spiralling out of control."

Kirsten thought about this. She grabbed the pen and sketched out a quick diagram, muttering, "Parasites. Food chains. Magical eco-systems. Mm, yeah, I see."

Hazel waited, patiently, trying not to let her eyes flick to the door.

"You may be right, Hazel." Kirsten spoke slowly. "Perhaps the lizards eat these little insects. And the fact that they have been removed... you may be right."

Wow. They must have been difficult words for her to say, Hazel thought, leg jiggling under the table.

"Hmm. The magical world is likely to have a delicate balance, where species are dependent on other species as well. I never took that into account. An interconnected community of supernatural organisms, all reliant on each other. More research may be needed."

"But this problem is happening right now. We've got to do something."

"Ecosystems can be rejuvenated," Kirsten said. "That is the wonderful and hopeful thing and the reason I got into Environmental Science in the first place. And I think we can bring this one back too."

"Will you put the creatures back where they rightfully live?"

Kirsten stared at her, no emotion at all on her face. It felt like minutes ticked by.

She finally nodded. Once. Hazel breathed out.

"I suppose I will have to." Kirsten folded her arms.

Hazel breathed a sigh of relief. She was making progress. She took a step towards the door so she didn't get caught in the crossfire when her cousin arrived.

"Now, Joel and Briar, you will forget," Kirsten said, and her voice echoed terribly around the room, "everything Hazel ever told you about me. Everything you saw and heard today."

"What?"

"And Hazel, you will stop. Still."

All of her muscles screamed as she came to a stop, leaning forward slightly, head turned to the side. She squeaked, but she couldn't look around.

"It is much easier to make people forget things than you'd think, Hazel. I actually learnt to do it on myself first. Something... terrible happened, when I was a kid. I wanted to forget and went rummaging through all of the magical books in our attic. That was where I first learnt about this little potion, actually, tucked in a recipe book, titled Margaret's Warming Drink."

Hazel managed to move her little finger.

Kirsten raised her voice. "What have you two heard about me?"

"Nothing," Briar and Joel intoned, and their voices chilled her to the bone.

"You can move now," Kirsten said with a smile.

Hazel fell forward suddenly, and she caught herself with her hands, gasping.

"Alright," she said, clearly. Bitterly.

"Alright what?"

How long was her cousin going to take? Hazel forced herself not to look at the door.

"I want... to join you."

Three faces turned to her in shock. Kirsten projected suspicion. Joel's happiness floated to her. Briar just pursed her lips.

"What other choice do I have?"

"Right choice, Hazel." Rummaging on her desk, Kirsten pulled out some papers and placed them in the centre of the table, laying a pen carefully on top.

She sat down in the chair and flicked through the papers, which were pre-printed with her full name and had a space to initial each page.

From behind her, Hazel heard the sound of footsteps running. Voices raised. Kirsten's eyes widened, as she looked to the doorway, then flicked to Hazel, uncertain.

A slight draught lifted Hazel's hair. She looked behind when she heard a deep voice among them. Along with Fritha, eyes narrowed in concentration, and Diana, looking magnificent in a bright orange dress, Hazel's ex, Hadley, was standing just inside the door.

"You—" they chanted.

"Silence," commanded Kirsten in that terrible voice. The voices stopped, and the three opened and closed their mouths.

"Oh dear," Kirsten said to Hazel. "What's all this about?"

Hazel stared back, defiant.

"Stop," commanded Kirsten, in that voice that echoed in the room, in her mind, behind her eyes.

"Do not move a muscle," Kirsten called, and every muscle in Hazel's body cramped painfully. She let out a small noise of pain. Hazel knew she was stronger than this. She just had to concentrate. She took herself back to the bridge in her mind.

"Sit."

Hazel sat, and her legs cramped. At the same moment, everyone else in the room sat. She felt completely alone. No-one was coming to save her. Everything was controlled by that voice.

She strained against the pain, until tears leaked from her eyes.

Then a face appeared, to her right. She flicked her eyes to the side to look at the transparent woman. A kind face, not too different from Hazel's own. It was Lavender. The ghost smiled a genuine smile, an encouraging smile, making Hazel realize that she knew what to do. Her aunt was brilliant!

Hazel started at Z. She thought of Y, then X. As she went through the alphabet backwards, it distracted her just enough to clear her mind. She felt her power pulsing back through her veins and gathered it together.

She stood up, slowly, and straightened her shoulders.

"You never found out the whole story, Kirsten. About our families."

Hazel chanted the spell, exactly as she had seen Lavender speak it in that chilly bedroom.

"You who take away their choice

We call on the wind to take

The power of your voice."

The past repeated itself, in patterns that were constructive but also sometimes destructive. Generations of people engaged in a dance they had no idea they had been dancing for centuries.

She repeated the chant, and the wind increased to a breeze, lifting dust in a whirlpool above the concrete floor.

Kirsten stepped forward and opened her mouth to say something, and she raised the volume.

Kirsten grabbed at her throat. When the third chant dropped away, silence fell, heavy and pregnant. Hazel couldn't look away. Kirsten dropped to her knees, and a moan escaped her lips.

The ghost of Lavender Redferne faded away, satisfied that her story had been told.

Hazel walked around the desk, and saw Kirsten's mouth moving. She brought her face close, wanting to help her. Hazel saw all the thoughts Kirsten had kept hidden until now. All the pain and hurt she had kept inside for a lifetime came gushing out.

"It was my brother," she gasped.

Hazel saw Kirsten as a young girl of about 11, bent over a little boy with messy, black hair. Timothy, Hazel remembered from the family tree.

If only he'd been able to stand up to his bullies, everything would be different.

Don't you know what it's like not to be able to save someone you love? And then you find out you have this ability and you work and work until you're powerful. But, by then, it's too late, and you have to spend every day of your life making up for it by giving a little bit of self-esteem to strangers who you don't really care about? But it is never enough.

She felt the resentment in Kirsten's parents' eyes, as the blame for the little boy's death came between them. Fell on the older sister who had arrived late. Guilt.

Guilt would cause the gaping blackness that she had noticed. The yawning hole that Kirsten had been trying to fill by helping others with the potion.

Imagine if he had had Confidence back then. Everything would have been different. What wouldn't you do to save the ones you love?

What would she do? Hazel reflected on everything she had done to get here. She'd pretended to be an old woman at the beauty salon. She'd stubbornly focused on learning what her ancestors had to tell her. She'd come here alone, although she was terrified, and risked her job. Breaking into a house. Lying. Taken away another witch's power. What wouldn't she do?

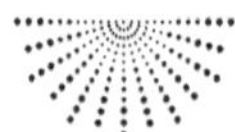

CHAPTER EIGHTEEN

*H*azel walked into the sea, ignoring the signs her body gave her that she was going to be paralysed with cold. When things got tough, she became restless, leaving the houses and streets behind, and was always drawn back to the sea.

Today, the sky was overcast and a few drops of rain fell on her as she ran down the beach. The wind whipped the waves into white foam. The prickling shock froze her limbs and her heart raced as all her blood was drawn to her core. She focused on a dab of gold and green far away, an island visible above the horizon.

Christo had called her into the office today at work and given her notice that her position would be made redundant. She had listened, numb, until she walked out the front doors. What would she do now? Who was she without her job?

A midwinter swim is good for the soul, she told herself, ducking her head under. She reached out, and found her stroke. It would be so easy to swim the pain away. To head for that little island. Then she stopped, treading water, tasting salt spray as the waves lapped around her neck. She thought of the one thing that pulled her back to land. Joel.

Hazel couldn't stand the distance between them anymore. She just wasn't sure how to bridge it. They had carefully avoided talking about everything that had happened at home, and Joel had kept himself busy with his hammer and nails any time he started thinking too much.

Joel and Briar had spent a day having a magical cleansing, much to Joel's feigned disgust. Briar told her later that he actually seemed to enjoy it. Then Fritha and Hazel took them out for lunch and told them everything that had happened. Briar was deeply ashamed that she had been so taken in by Kirsten. Joel immediately went into a deep depression, a black void where Hazel felt she could hardly reach him.

Hazel flipped onto her back and kicked herself along until she was touching the sand in the shallows. She dug her fingers into the sand. A piece of driftwood stuck out of the water and she tried to pick it up, but it was much larger and heavier than it seemed. She felt under the water that it was actually a log, about two metres long, and the piece that stuck out of the water was just a twig on the side of it..

She dragged herself up the beach, the cold wind whipping sand at her skin like tiny darts, and reached for her towel.

After a shower, she snuck into the bedroom and opened Joel's top drawer. She found the boxer shorts with the bats and rolled them into a ball in her pocket. Next, she went over to her wardrobe and got out the blue dress she had worn on their first real date.

She hung the dress on its hanger in the hall, placed the boxers casually on the top of the laundry basket, and bent down to light the fire. Once it was crackling merrily, she pulled out her phone and searched for a recipe.

Joel had been thinking about the bad long enough. But that was just the tip of the branch. There was a lot more to their relationship and the stage was set to remind him of all the good things.

———

"In here," she called, when she heard Joel come in the front door.

"What's your dress doing out there?" he asked, standing in the doorway to the kitchen.

She blinked. Wow. That was the first thing he said to her?

"Ah, I put it there so I remember to take it to the dry cleaners," she said, getting out two matching plates from the cupboard.

His nose twitched. "What's that smell?"

"I hope you're hungry." She scraped a pale pile of food onto each plate and covered it with maple syrup.

"You... made pancakes?"

"Look, it's my first time. They don't look pretty," she said. "And I obviously had the pan at the wrong temperature. But I tried."

"Itsh good," he said, shovelling a huge forkful into his mouth. "Is that bacon?"

"Yup." Hazel sat down and took a bite. She could only taste a little bit of the burnt flavour, under all that syrup. What he didn't know was that she had added a few drops of honeysuckle essence to the pancake mixture, for truth, desire and interest in the present. A little help couldn't hurt in a case like this.

She knew he had been feeling guilty about what he had

done. She could see it, and almost feel the guilt's presence in the house, seeping between them, lengthening silences.

"How are you?" she asked him.

"Okay, I guess," he said, mopping up the sauce with the last bit of pancake.

"Are you?" she asked in reply, searching his face. "I'm not. I'm really not. Shall we go and sit in the lounge to talk? It's more comfortable."

"Sure."

He followed Hazel out of the kitchen, and she sunk down on the couch.

"Well, we got your land back," she said. "Let's focus on the positive."

Joel shrugged. "The Redfernes own the land," he said. "Not me."

Once Kirsten had lost the power of her voice, Hazel had negotiated with her to sign an agreement to sell the land back to the Redferne family for the same amount it was purchased for. Briar and Hazel's parents were happy to put in some money to purchase the section under a Family Trust. They ignored the strange looks their lawyer gave them when they asked for it to be called 'The Redferne Coven Trust'.

"You can be an honorary Redferne," she said to Joel. "You have the courage."

"I haven't though, have I? One little challenge and I went looking for the easy way."

"You've got it," she said, firmly. "You once helped me with a body even though you were terrified."

He took a deep breath. "The truth is... "

"I know," she said, softly.

"I guess you do," he said, looking at her like she had grown an extra head. "I guess you know what I'm feeling better than I do. But it helps me to say it. I have been feeling a lot of pressure to provide for you. Not just in terms of money, but being the sort of person you need me to be."

"I don't need— "

"Well, maybe it's just me. But I don't think I'm good enough for you. You're successful and driven. You go off fighting monsters and running meetings. Meanwhile, I'm here like some rescue dog that needs saving. And don't say that I'm not, because I know you love helping people more than anything."

Bonnie sat up. Hazel knew she was listening.

Joel got up and stared out the window, looking out at the tiny house that was taking shape in the backyard, its roof almost finished. She stood next to him and let her hand hang so that her finger was touching his. A tiny bridge between them.

"You built that," she said, "and the potion is not some superpower. It only helps you be more confident in what you already have."

"Don't be so nice about it," he said, a scowl on his face. "I let you down. And it's not even the first time. I led you into danger. I ignored what you had been telling me. All just because I wanted a stupid loan."

Black and grey energy emanated from him in waves.

"When I first met you, maybe I did want to help you. You were in a bad way. But after that, it was just so easy. I felt like I'd known you my whole life. At the same time, I want to know you better."

Hazel reached for his hand, pouring healing thoughts into her touch as she stroked his finger.

"You made a mistake at the start, and that woman took advantage. I think she could only do that because you are someone who wants to believe the best about people. So when she kept telling you to forget everything bad you knew about her, your mind did so.”

“Anyone could be taken in by her,” Hazel continued. “Even my aunt, a senior witch in the coven. That is what made it so perfect. Fear makes us do stupid things.”

“Yeah,” Joel said, then turned to her. “What was she whispering?”

“When?”

“At the end, you said Kirsten’s mouth was moving when you went over.”

“I can’t be sure, but I think she said, ‘Forget, Hazel.’”

“That was what she was thinking of just before her powers got taken away?” He made a disgusted noise.

“It didn’t work,” she said gently. “And it would have been fine if it did, because the others were there. As long as one person remembers, nothing can be forgotten.”

“It’s all my fault,” Joel said again.

“I can tell you feel really bad about it,” she said. “But it’s alright.”

“I am your greatest weakness. I... should probably leave.”

Tears pricked at her eyes. “No, I think it’s my tendency to be a bloody hero. And an idiot,” she laughed, and sniffed. “You don’t have to leave. And I don’t think you want to.”

“You’re always going to be at risk from me.”

“No, I’m not. You’re not going to do that again.” She blurted it, as if speaking made it the truth. Why didn’t he believe that? Why did she have to say it for him?

He turned to her and pulled her close, his arms warm and strong around her. “Wouldn’t you rather have someone who could be the strong, silent type?”

“I’d rather have you, you big idiot,” she said, into his chest.

"You've lost your job, and I know how much you loved that job." He stroked her hair.

"I've been thinking about that," she said, after a long pause. "There are other jobs. I mean, I don't know if I'd want to work with Kirsten anymore, even if I could."

Her aunt was not disappointed she'd lost her job. "You'll have time to be an elder witch. I just had a call from one of your cousins who needs some help with her powers," she had said. "You'd be perfect."

Hazel liked that idea, but also liked the thought of heading in a completely new direction.

"I might start up an agency, working with small businesses, plumbers and the like, helping them with their promotion. What do you think?"

Joel looked surprised. "You'd be good at that. You might have to deal with thickos like me, though."

"Yeah, that is my biggest issue," she joked, then looked at him seriously. "Hey, I know you didn't want to hurt me."

"Of course I didn't," he said, roughly. "I never would, Red."

He knew she didn't want to hurt her. But Hazel found that the pain of being the only one who believed in their relationship stung more than any betrayal.

CHAPTER NINETEEN

It was another week until she saw the change in him. One day, he got up early, and when Hazel came out of the bedroom, she found him surrounded by boxes and tools in the hallway. For a moment, she thought he was leaving and she froze.

He stood up then and went back to repainting the door frame where the mushrooms had grown. A picture of an Egyptian pyramid hung in the hall and a new mat sat by the front door. 'You're beery welcome,' it said.

He did a half smile at her when he heard the floorboards creak. "Morning, beautiful," he said.

"It is a beautiful morning,"she replied, carefully. "What's all this?"

"I'm getting stuff done."

"Great," she said. "Not too sure about the doormat, though."

"No?"

"No," she replied. Maybe in a student flat, but not in a house. "Sorry."

"I've unpacked a few of my things. Made it a bit more

homely."

"Good." Hazel looked at the door frame, shiny with wet paint.

"Come here," he said, and pulled the door open. "But carefully."

She slipped through the door, pulling her dressing gown around her. Frost shimmered on the ground outside as the sun shone in a clear blue sky. It was going to be a lovely day.

The porch was a little slippery, and Joel put his arms around her. She could hear his heart beating strongly next to her ear.

The door was shiny with wet paint in a bright red. The horse knocker she loved had been refastened in the middle of the door and new wooden planters were affixed beneath the windows.

"You can plant those out in spring. Or we can. Together," he said, gesturing to the planters.

"You did all this this morning?"

"And last night. Do you like the colour? I ran it past Grannie Em first."

"You did? It's perfect." Hazel noticed the vines on the house seemed to be flourishing, growing up and around the windows, encircling the house like protective arms. The trees, plants, the insect life felt right now. It felt alive.

The ground vibrated beneath her feet, as the life force pulsed, slow and steady. Roots reached out. Plants and people grew and changed, infinitely slowly. But she was listening.

"What brought this on?"

"Well, it came to me when I was working yesterday," he said. "A piece of wood, when I hold it in my hand, is just wood, until I see what it is going to be. Then it becomes something special."

He held her tight. "And it made me think about how you

always see me as such a good person. You forgave me without a question, when I totally let you down. I left you when you were having the vision, asked you to come and pick me up. You even forgave the fact I went behind your back to get the potion. So I should be able to forgive myself."

"I know what's in here," she said, tapping his chest with her palm. "That's why I can forgive so easily."

He held her close and kissed her hair, her forehead, her nose.

"I've fought so hard with myself about loving you, because I felt like I was less. But I needed a kick in the pants. From now on, I'm going to make us what I want it to be. See it in the best light. Like you always have."

He lifted her chin up and kissed her deeply, shame and guilt melting away, until only the present moment remained.

Maybe this was what love was. She thought about the hard conversations, difficult truths and feelings that cut like a knife. Maybe it was being open enough that you could hurt each other and be hurt, but trusting that you wouldn't.

"You don't want to leave?"

"No, I don't want to leave. I want to stay. Hang around like a bad smell."

Maybe it was that feeling of not quite knowing someone, no matter how long you spent with them, or how much you tried to read them. But *wanting* to know them completely.

Then again, perhaps it was more simple than that. Like pancakes for dinner with a glass of wine. Lying on the grass beneath the trees. Kissing under a skylight full of stars. Getting caught up in each other's adventures.

That was enough.

The End

A NOTE FROM K M JACKWAYS

I hope you enjoyed Murmurs of Magic. I hope to share more about these characters in future books. I'm also working on a paranormal cosy mystery called Murder for a Song. Please sign up to the newsletter to find out about new releases.

If you liked Murmurs of Magic, please consider reviewing it on Amazon or Goodreads. Every review helps!

Want more witchy fiction? If you'd like to find out more about us and our books, check out our website at www.witchyfiction.com

ABOUT THE AUTHOR

K M Jackways is a freelance writer and mother of two based in Canterbury. She loves shady green places and teaching animals to talk. Her fiction has been published in various magazines and anthologies, including The Best Small Fictions 2019 and Takahē Magazine. She has lived in random places, from Dunedin, New Zealand, to Bordeaux in France. Her stories expose the hidden lives of the past and the future, inspired by her background in psychology and linguistics.

MORE WITCHY FICTION BOOKS

Need more witchy goodness in your life? Check out the full list of Witchy Fiction books below!

Holloway Witches, by Isa Pearl Ritchie: Ursula escapes to Holloway Road leaving her former life in tatters following a bad break-up. She's looking forward to a quiet respite in a cozy cottage with a lush garden and lots of bookshelves, but instead she can't shake the eerie feeling she's being followed...

Familiars and Foes, by Helen Vivienne Fletcher: Adeline yearns for family, but for years, the closest she's gotten is her assistance dog, Coco. When a frightening encounter with a ghost brings an old friend back into her life, it seems like Adeline's about to find the companionship she's been missing. But her crush might have to wait. As the ghost's smoky presence increases, Adeline feels its hold on those around her tightening dangerously.

Overdues and Occultism, by Jamie Sands: That Basil is a librarian comes as no surprise to his Mt Eden community. That he's a witch? Yeah. That might raise more than a few eyebrows. When Sebastian, a paranormal investigator filming a web series starts snooping around Basil's library, he stirs up more than just Basil's heart.

Riverwitch, by Rem Wigmore: Self-taught witch Ashley Robinson spends most of her time on community work and picking up litter. When something goes badly wrong with the Waikato River, Ash is determined to get to the bottom of it. If only Bryony Manu, the other witch in town, could put aside their arrogance to help.

Jingle Spells: A mysterious child is spotted swimming far from the beach. A woman searches for a ghost in a blacked out hospital. One witch introduces her lover to her family, while another takes care of a magicaholic baby dolphin in her boyfriend's absence. A young man bonds with his pet eel, and yarnbombers accidentally summon something otherworldly. Jingle Spells is a collection of fun, quirky, and witchily magical Christmas stories by seven Witchy Fiction authors.

Microscopes and Magic (Windflower Two), by Andi C. Buchanan: Marigold Nightfield's life changed when she absorbed the magic stored in a family heirloom. Now, she's part of a growing network of magic-working scientists who are trying to change the world for the better, and has a girlfriend from a sprawling, powerful, witchy family. But when her girlfriend's work is destroyed by possible sabotage, and strange things start appearing in Wellington's green belt, Marigold's amazing new life starts to unravel. She'll have to not only draw on her scientific background and magical abilities, but make new connections and grow in confidence to face this new threat.

A Gap in the Veil, by Sam Schenk: As a mechanic, Greg can fix just about anything—except his broken heart. When a visiting musician dials up the charm after a gig in town, Greg's life looks to be taking a turn for the better. His plans to keep things simple between them are complicated by the awakening of a spirit bent on corruption. Greg must make choices between appearing distant or bringing his new friend into the fight, all the while saving Wellington from a past it had almost forgotten.

Succulents and Spells (Windflower One), by Andi C. Buchanan: Laurel Windflower is a witch from a family of magic workers - but her own life is going nowhere until Marigold Nightfield knocks on her door. Marigold is a scientist from a family of witches, and she's in search of monsters. What lies ahead could reveal all Laurel's shortcomings to the woman she's trying to impress... or uncover the true nature of her power.

Hexes & Vexes, by Nova Blake: Small towns are full of gossip, and Mia is pretty sure that no one in her hometown of Okato has ever stopped talking about her. Cast off by her best friend, blamed for a local tragedy – Mia had no choice but to run away.

Now, ten years later, she's being dragged back.

Witching with Dolphins, by Janna Ruth: Friends before magic (or boys) has always been Harper's prerogative. Her best friend Valerie is everything she is not: beautiful, confident, and the most powerful witch on Banks Peninsula. They might not see eye to eye on everything, yet, when a sinister scientist threatens their coven, Harper is willing to give up everything: the man they both love, her life, or even the little magic she has.

Raven's Haven for Women of Magic, by Anna Kirtlan: Cassandra Frost has zero interest in fortune-telling or brewing foul-smelling things in cauldrons, and much prefers the company of non-magical folk. She does her best to keep her powers under wraps to protect the secrecy of the Wellington witching community. But that's easier said than done when your grandmother lives in Raven's Haven for Women of Magic. Magical fireworks, mobility broom races and irresponsible use of cat litter spells are all part of the game for the witching retirement village residents. When Cassandra's forced to cast a spell in the open to save Adrian, a geeky graphic designer with secrets of his own, her two worlds spectacularly collide, and she learns the Haven is much more than meets the eye.

Potions & Promotions (Redferne Witches, Prequel)

Brand of Magic (Redferne Witches, Book 1)

Boundless Magic (Redferne Witches, Book 2)

Murmurs of Magic (Redferne Witches, Book 3)